the calling

BOOK ONE

DEFENDERS OF THE REALMS

the calling

by

NATHAN D THOMAS

Also By Nathan D. Thomas

Be Confident in Your Creation

Be Confident in Your Calling

What's Stopping You?

Library of Congress Cataloging - in Publication Data
Thomas, Nathan D, author.
    The Calling/Nathan D Thomas
    Defenders of the Realms Series Book One

ISBN-13: 978-1508733874
ISBN-10: 1508733872
Young Adult Christian Fiction/Fantasy
Library of Congress Control Number 2015903602

Printed in South Carolina, the United States of America

This book is dedicated to

Grace

Toby

Milo

Vander

and Wren Thomas.

May you all find your identity

as defenders of the King.

table of contents

introduction:
find your story

What you are about to read is fiction, but it is also real. The people found in these stories are made up, and yet they make up all of us reading this book. The story found on the pages of this book is my story; I authored it, and yet it is your story because you live it. This book is like so many other books written throughout history, and yet it is unlike any book written for hundreds of years.

This book is unique because though the story is fiction, the underlying elements of this book come from the Bible and are elements found in your life. All the adventures, experiences, obstacles, and victories the characters in these stories face are adventures, experiences, obstacles, and victories you too experience, struggle with, and enjoy in your spiritual life.

You may never have the opportunity to travel between realms, have conversations with angels, stare down the Enemy in person, or travel through portals. You may never have to enter the room of fire, the room of thorns, the room of the Enemy, or the last room; but for you to grasp the helmet of salvation and live a Christian life that is pleasing to the Lord, you will have to do battle with the real enemies portrayed in these stories. This book offers you the ability to understand your enemies and see the path of victory as given by the teachings of the Bible.

So let me encourage you to find your story in this book. Discover your identity in Jesus Christ as a defender of the realms. Wage war against the Enemy and his servants as they attempt to destroy your life in the physical realm, and find real life help to gain the real victories in this war through the following of Elijah's adventures. This book is much more than a book; it is a weapon that God can use to make the Scriptures come alive in your life.

I pray that you will enjoy this story, but more than that, I pray that this story will challenge you to find your own story and identity in Jesus Christ. Enjoy reading and keep an eye out for the next installment of the

Defenders of the Realms.

chapter 1
the history

In a time before time existed, in a realm far superior to the physical realm we dwell in today, life was perfect. Life was perfect because the Creator was perfect and in the presence of His perfection, all things dwelt. In the Creator's presence there was no need for a sun, moon, stars, or any source of light or life, for the Thrice-Holy God was the source of light and life, and His light and life encompassed all things.

In this complete state of perfection, the Thrice-Holy God gave life to countless ministers and filled the lives of these ministers with unspeakable joy. Every moment of existence was filled with the worship of the King and the fellowshipping of His ministers. There was no sin, no death, no pain, no sorrow, or any idea what any of these things were.

Among those the King gave life were several ministers of supreme beauty: Michael, a great warrior; Gabriel, a great messenger; and Lucifer, a beautiful musician. All of the ministers served with great love and worship, but it was Lucifer whose gifts and service allowed him access to walk up and down through the sacred stones of fire. As the worship ascended to the throne of the King, the King would send declaration after declaration of love, joy, and peace to all corners of existence. These declarations from the King filled the ministers with unspeakable satisfaction that they thanked the King for by bestowing upon Him even more worship and honor.

This was perfection, and this perfect state of absolute completeness was what the King desired all of His creation to know. But this state of perfection did not remain eternally. One day as the worship continued, the King's voice sounded throughout the realm calling Lucifer to enter His presence. The entire realm stopped their worship and in silence looked to see what was happening, because the voice of the King was not the voice of purest joy they knew. The King's voice was a voice of deep agony, an emotion they would encounter for the first time that day. Instruments of praise fell to the ground as the ministers of the King witnessed Lucifer's appearance.

The perfectly beautiful creation of the King, created to lift up, worship, magnify, and honor the King, did not radiate with the joy and happiness he had since the day of his creation, but radiated another new emotion: anger. The elevated minister approached the throne of the King, but not with joy. Lucifer stumbled and shielded his eyes as he approached and reacted in such a way it appeared as if he was fighting the command of the King to approach. With a face twisted by anger the elevated minister reluctantly knelt before his King.

As all of creation silently watched, the King spoke to Lucifer. "Thus says the Lord GOD: You were the seal of perfection, full of wisdom and perfect in beauty. You were in Eden, the garden of God. Every precious stone was your covering: the sardius, topaz, and diamond, beryl, onyx, and jasper, sapphire, turquoise, and emerald with gold. The workmanship of your timbrels and pipes was prepared for you on the day you were created. You were the anointed cherub who covers; I established you. You were on the holy mountain of God; you walked back and forth in the midst of fiery stones. You were perfect in your ways from the day you were created, till iniquity was found in you...therefore I cast you as a profane thing out of the mountain of God; and I destroyed you, O covering cherub, from the midst of the fiery stones."

All of creation gasped. Many cried out in confusion, having never witnessed any form of sin, rebellion, or condemnation. Lucifer, now known as the Enemy, did not seem shocked or remorseful, but rather smiled a twisted smile and called out for aid. To the devastating surprise of all the faithful ministers of the King, one-third of all the King's ministers rose to aid the Enemy in his attempt to overthrow the King. The other ministers, led by Michael, rose to defend the King but were stopped by the command of the King. Understand that the King is all-knowing, and was not surprised by the call of the Enemy or by the one-third of His beloved creation that rose against Him.

The Enemy thought he had a chance, but the Enemy never understood the true power and might of the King. In a voice now more full of pain than creation had ever heard, and a voice so full of pain that it would only be rivaled by a voice calling out from a cross in the future, the King condemned both the Enemy and the rebellious ministers to a future in the Lake of Fire. Then with only the words of His mouth, the King cast the Enemy and the rebellious ministers out of His presence.

Defeated and destitute, the Enemy allowed his rage to consume his entire being. Rallying his followers, the Enemy declared war on the King and vowed vengeance against the God who banished him. But the Enemy knew he could not touch the King, and so he waited for an opportunity to wage his war.

That opportunity came, as the King once again created the miracle of life. This time, however, the King created life in the physical realm to the creatures of the earth and to His beloved mankind. The Enemy watched and saw the King place upon these weak creatures His perfect love, joy, and peace. Seeing an opportunity to strike at the heart of the King, the Enemy focused his war on the destruction of man.

Once again, the Enemy corrupted the King's environment of perfection as he tempted man in the garden. Man fell to the workings of the Enemy as sin and death were now introduced to the King's beloved creatures. Grieved by the fall of man, the King, who knew this would happen, set forth His plan of ultimate victory, the plan of redemption.

"I will put enmity," decreed the King to the Enemy, "between you and the woman, and between your offspring and hers. He will crush your head, and you will strike His heel."

The King's plan of redemption gained the ultimate victory over the Enemy when the King Himself came to earth and paid the penalty for the sin of all man. The King triumphed over the Enemy and publicly announced His victory when a pained voiced echoed throughout creation, "It is finished." Three days later, the King rose with the keys of hell and death in His possession and the Enemy defeated for all eternity. At that time, the Enemy's doom was sealed; however, the King has seen fit to allow the battle to continue for a time.

One day the redemptive work of Jesus Christ will come full circle and creation will be restored to a state of perfection. But that time has not come yet. From the time of the Garden of Eden to the present, God has called and empowered humans to fight the Enemy and claim great victories and glory for the King. Many great warriors have arisen through the years, but their time has ended.

Today the battle wages for the souls of man. The Enemy who knows his time is short is seeking to devour as many of the King's beloved creation as possible. The King is calling out to all His creation and His eyes are scanning to see if there are any who love Him enough to answer the call and take up the title of defender of the realms.

chapter 2
a morning of memory

The alarm clock rang, dragging Eli out of a night of tumultuous sleep. Thankful to be free from the scenes that haunted his dreams, Eli slowly reached over, hit the snooze button, and lay back down. Closing his eyes, hoping for a few minutes of peaceful sleep, Eli was immediately revisited by his nightmares about the events of the day ahead. Giving up on sleep, Eli opened his eyes and, seeing rays of morning light flooding in through cracks in his curtain, was forced to admit that the day he had dreaded had finally arrived.

He paused for a moment and watched the dust particles glide through the rays of light. They looked so tranquil, so at peace, and they reminded Eli of the many mornings in which he woke in this room excited to see the light. Eli wished with all of his might that today was one of those days. The snooze alarm broke the silence and shook Eli out of his thoughts. With a quick swipe of his hand, Eli picked up the alarm clock and slammed it against the table. The alarm stopped, but Eli did not. Overcome by the emotions stirred by the day's arrival, he continued to hit the alarm clock on his night stand until the screen cracked and the digital numbers disappeared. The sight of the broken clock in his grandfather's house replaced Eli's anger with sadness. Eli clinched his eyes shut attempting to fend off the tears, but it was too late. Sitting in bed looking at the broken clock, Eli began to cry.

Eli was not an emotional kid. Before these past few weeks, he could count the number of times he cried, including the times Eli was legitimately injured, on one hand. Eli always prided himself on how tough he was, but all that toughness melted away this past month. It was only a few weeks ago that Eli learned that his grandfather, one of his best friends, had only a short time to live. The doctor said the cancer was advanced, whatever that meant, and there was nothing they could do. But they said it would be months, not weeks, before his grandfather would die. Nevertheless, here Eli was, sitting up in a room he frequented in the house of his grandfather who "passed away," what his parents called his grandfather's death, a few days ago.

No, thought Eli. *He did not "pass away." He's dead, gone forever, never coming back!*

Warm tears continued their trek down the sides of Eli's face. He would have loved to lie back down and sleep the hours away until the sting of his grandfather's death passed, but he knew he had to get ready for the funeral.

With a grunt of determination to get this day over with, Eli threw off his covers, sat on the edge of the bed and wiped his tears.

"I hate funerals," mumbled Eli as he slouched over on the side of the bed.

Eli had not been to a lot of funerals, but the ones he had attended left him with a terrible dislike for all funerals. Funerals contained three of the things Eli hated most: crying people, dead bodies, and sermons on heaven and hell. Eli did not know which part about his grandfather's funeral would bother him the most: seeing his grandfather in a casket, or hearing another sermon on heaven and hell.

The thought of his grandfather lying in a casket stuck in Eli's mind. Eli clinched his eyes and shook his head to rid his mind of this picture as a few more tears squeezed out of the sides of his eyes.

Growing up in church, Eli had heard many salvation messages and knew what the Bible taught about how a person can go to heaven. Eli said a prayer a long time ago, but he knew that it was mainly to please his parents and Sunday school teacher, Mrs. Finley. It was not that Eli did not want to be saved, but he just wanted to see what the world was like before committing to all the rules of Christianity.

Eli loved adventure, just like his grandfather. He loved to listen to the many adventures his grandfather experienced in life. From war stories to stories about his grandfather's truck-driving days, Eli could not get enough of all there was to experience in life. Wanting to have his own adventures in life, Eli was sure that if he became a Christian, God would not allow him to have a fun life but would require him to live a boring life of rules and regulations.

Memories of listening to his grandfather's incredible adventures as they sat and ate pancakes flooded Eli's mind. Their shared love for adventure and excitement was one reason Eli and his grandfather were so much closer than Eli and the rest of his family.

Their unique closeness started to change about five years earlier, when Eli's grandmother died suddenly. Her death caused his grandfather to go into a deep depression. To cope with his depression, Eli's grandfather drank a lot more than he used to and pulled away from all relationships.

Eli witnessed his grandfather do a lot of things that only seemed to add to his grandfather's depression, but one day, his grandfather did something Eli never expected to see his grandfather do: he went to church. His grandfather's attendance was the first of many surprises that day for Eli. That day was the first day that Eli could remember his grandfather carrying a Bible. At the end of the service, Eli's grandfather walked down the auditorium aisle and talked with the pastor. That morning, Eli's grandfather accepted Christ and that night, Eli's grandfather was baptized. From that day on, things changed.

After his salvation, Eli's grandfather stopped drinking, smoking, and cursing. No longer did his grandfather tell the stories of his truck-driving days like he used to, but rather, talked about the Bible. His grandfather, who used to spend his days playing pool and poker, was now always at the nursing homes or homeless missions talking with people and sharing Jesus Christ. Every Sunday, Eli knew his grandfather would be attending the Church of the Open Door, the small church Eli's grandmother attended before she died, talking to everyone he could and yelling "Amen!" at the top of his lungs.

Perhaps the most drastic change occurred in the way he talked with Eli. He did not make fun of church stuff and Christians anymore, but rather talked about his "new life" like it was one of his adventures. He even told Eli that the past five years had been the greatest adventure he had ever known. This change in his grandfather's attitude came with a constant desire to talk with Eli about his own salvation. Eli knew his grandfather understood his heart better than anyone else. As a result, Eli began to spend less and less time at his grandfather's house and with his grandfather on the weekends. Even though his grandfather lived just on the outskirts of the same town, Eli kept producing excuses as to why he could not go over and spend time with him. It was not until his parents sat him down and explained what the doctors told them that Eli did not want to leave his grandfather's side.

He could remember his father telling him, "Eli, Grandpa called about his doctor's visit. Son, your grandfather has advanced cancer. The doctors told him he has only about six months to live."

Eli never recovered from the news of his grandfather's cancer because instead of six months, Eli's grandfather died in a mere two weeks.

Eli placed his head in his hands and rubbed his hands up his face and through his hair as if to rub all these memories out of his mind.

I would give anything, thought Eli, *to not have all of these memories going through my head constantly.*

After closing his eyes and squeezing them shut in an attempt to clear his mind, Eli opened his eyes and stared at his funeral outfit hanging in his closet.

Fine, thought Eli. *I guess I have to get dressed at some point. I don't think even grandpa would find it funny if I showed up in my underwear.*

Eli laughed to himself, but instead of making him feel better, thinking about his grandfather's sense of humor only made him feel worse.

He removed the white button-up shirt and the black suit from the door and successfully navigated the process of putting them on. Having finished his task, including wearing matching black socks and shoes for probably the first time in his life, Eli walked over to the full-length mirror in the room.

Eli was average size for a fourteen-year-old, around five-foot-three with a medium build on the muscular side. Eli had always been proud of his muscles, and working out was a hobby he shared with his grandfather. Though Eli never told his grandfather, his grandfather's incredible health and strength always made Eli want to be just like him.

"Boy are you lucky," Eli remembered his grandfather saying this past Easter when they were all getting ready for family pictures.

"What do you mean, Grandpa?"

"Well, son, not too many people can claim to look like one of the most dashing men on the planet. You are truly blessed. Don't tell your dad this, but I am pretty sure your last name should be Granite not Storm."

"Yep," said Eli as he fondly remembered his grandfather teasing about his last name. "I am definitely a Granite."

Once Eli was dressed, he looked again at the mirror to check on the status of his hair. His dirty-blonde hair shone in the mirror as the sunlight from the window shined directly behind him. Eli sprayed his hair down a little with his spray bottle, rubbed some hair gel in it, and formed his familiar spiked-up-in-the-front hairstyle.

All that was left for Eli to finish before going down to breakfast was tying his black tie. Fumbling around for several minutes, Eli was reminded that there were only a few things in life he hated more than wearing ties: school, school work, devastating physical pain, and his mother's experimental dinners.

That's a good point, thought Eli. *I had to brush my teeth three times to get the flavor of mom's experimental "organic" hamburgers out of my mouth.*

Eli shuddered as he remembered the taste of the hamburgers and then laughed as he remembered his mother catching his grandfather trying to feed his organic hamburger to the dog. With his tie all finished, Eli looked in the mirror one last time.

"Well, Grandpa, it looks like I'm all dressed up to tell you goodbye."

Eli closed his eyes as a fresh set of tears slowly rolled down his cheeks. Wiping his tears, Eli walked over to the door and exited his room.

Eli's grandfather's house was a two-story, cape-cod style home that faced west into the town. The second story of the house had two bedrooms, each on opposite sides of the hallway from each other, and a bathroom situated in the center of the hallway just opposite the staircase that connected the lower story. Eli's room was upstairs to the left. Years ago when Eli's grandfather gave him the choice of which room he would like to stay in when he visited, Eli chose this room because when he stepped out of his room he was welcomed by a wall full of pictures. There were pictures of Eli's grandparents when they were children, in high school, college, and as adults. Mixed in the pictures were pictures of Eli's parents and uncles, as well as pictures of Eli's memories with his grandparents.

This morning, however, the wall of pictures that used to be a comfort and source of joy to Eli was just another reminder to him that his grandfather, whom he loved and admired so much, was nothing more than a memory. This morning, the pictures on the wall only made Eli angry at his parents' decision to stay in his grandfather's house before the funeral.

Your uncles and cousins will be staying at our house, and so we will be staying at Dad's house before the funeral, Eli recited his mother's words in a mocking tone in his mind. *You have spent lots of time there and hopefully it will help you remember the good times you spent with Dad.*

"Whatever," said Eli aloud as reached the bottom of the stairs, turned right, and walked into the kitchen.

"Good morning, Elijah," his mother said in a voice Eli thought way to cheery considering the circumstances.

Eli looked up at his mother and noticed she was wearing a black dress with black shoes and a black hat. Eli could tell that his mother had been crying, but that did not keep him from responding angrily.

"What's so good about it, Mom? And I told you, I want to be called Eli."

Eli never liked his name. He knew it came from the Bible, and he knew a lot of his friends knew it came from the Bible. In his mind, a Bible name made him look like some dorky Christian boy from a dorky Christian family.

"Well, okay, *Eli*," said his mom with care in her voice. "I made you some pancakes."

Eli sat down across from his father and began to stick the butter knife into the butter acting like he was killing something.

"Good morning, Son. How did you sleep?" asked Eli's dad, looking amused at Eli's attack on the butter.

"How did I sleep?" retorted Eli. "What is wrong with you guys? Mom is acting chipper and you ask me how I slept! Don't you know what today is? Am I the only one who is going to miss Grandpa?"

Eli's mother held Eli's pancakes in mid air between the pan and Eli's plate with a grief stricken look on her face. Eli knew he had hurt her, but refused to feel guilty.

"Eli, we are all going to miss Grandpa, especially your mother," started his father. "But Grandpa was a Christian and is in heaven. This helps make today easier."

Not wanting to find himself in another discussion about his salvation, Eli grunted in agreement then focused on fixing and eating his pancakes.

After finishing breakfast, Eli sat at the dining table staring at the morning's newspaper without actually reading it until his dad walked over and said what Eli had been dreading to hear all morning. "Come on, Eli, it's time to go to the funeral."

chapter 3
the funeral

Hearing his dad's words made Eli feel short of breath, as if someone had just sucked all the oxygen out of the room. Overcome with a sense of dread, Eli slowly trudged outside and loaded up in his family's sedan. Hoping somehow the short trip to his grandfather's church would miraculously take hours, Eli once again had difficulty breathing as the car turned the corner and the Open Door Church came into view.

The Open Door Church was an old church full of mostly old people. The building was at least fifty years old and had seen better days. The building, which resembled the letter "T" was mainly just an auditorium with two little areas behind the baptismal for classes. Eli's family used to come when he was younger and attend the Open Door Church with his grandmother before deciding to attend Grace Gospel Fellowship, another church in town that emphasized family ministries the Open Door Church could not provide.

Though Eli did have some fond memories of the Open Door Church, he could not get over the memories of his grandmother's funeral held at this church almost five years ago to the date. Eli would never forget the feeling of seeing his grandfather sobbing uncontrollably throughout the entire ceremony. The memories from that day caused Eli to loathe the sight of the building.

After his dad parked the car, the family unloaded and walked into the building. Welcomed by the familiar odor of Pledge and library books, Eli concluded that everything was the same as it was five years ago; only this time, it was his best friend in the casket.

"I hate this church," Eli mumbled as he braced himself for another day of sorrow which would be forever linked to this building.

Eli stood in the doorway to the church and watched as the funeral guests arrived. Eli's grandfather's godless lifestyle for most of his life was evident in Eli's uncles. Two of Eli's uncles had drinking problems that resulted in at least one divorce apiece as well as countless other health and social issues. Eli's cousins, resulting from those tumultuous relationships, were so ill-behaved that not even Eli found their antics humorous (and that was saying something). The only member of his mother's family that Eli respected was his Uncle Douglas, who also happened to be the source of Eli's middle name.

Douglas was a large muscular man who resembled Eli's grandfather in many ways. A single man, Doug was well tempered and Eli always enjoyed the time he was able to spend in Doug's company. In many ways, Eli felt more like Doug's younger brother than he did Doug's nephew. Doug was also one of the only family members who stood by Eli's grandfather after the death of Eli's grandmother—something for which Eli would be forever grateful.

Along with the motley crew that was his extended family, a large number of other guests arrived and took their place in the auditorium. Amazed at the large number of people in attendance, Eli walked over to his dad.

"Hey, Dad," whispered Eli. "Who are all these people?"

"These are just some of the people your grandfather worked with at the nursing homes and missions."

"Okay," replied Eli as he thought for a moment. "If more people show up, do you think we will have to move the funeral over to our church?"

"No, Son," his dad replied. "There will be enough room here. Besides, your grandfather loved this church. One of his last requests was to have the funeral here."

"Okay, just checking," was Eli's reply as he continued to watch the happenings all around him.

All in all, Eli thought things were going better than he expected when suddenly his world got turned upside-down. At that moment, the funeral home arrived and wheeled in the casket. Eli froze in place and he was sure time had slowed down. Eli could no longer hear any chatter or see anything other than the casket carrying the body of his grandfather, his best friend, through the doors and down the worn carpet aisle. Eli watched the men position the casket below the pulpit and open the head of the casket revealing his grandfather's face.

That was all Eli could take. He ran to the bathroom not wanting anyone to see what was coming. Eli rushed into the bathroom, slammed the door of the stall, sat down, and began to sob. Never had Eli been so overcome with emotions.

Gone forever! Eli yelled in his mind. *Grandpa is gone forever!*

Through his sobbing, Eli could hear others talking about him and he knew his father would soon be coming in to find him. Gathering all his strength, Eli wiped his eyes once more with the back of his hand, blew his nose with some toilet paper, and walked out to the funeral.

The music started up and he was seated with the family. After a few songs, sung by an auditorium of crying people, the pastor stood up in the pulpit. Eli began his familiar tactic of zoning out so as not to hear the sermon, when the pastor made an announcement that shocked Eli.

"Today," the pastor announced, "I am not going to preach a sermon that I wrote. I am going to preach a sermon written by David J. Granite."

Shocked by what he heard, Eli sat up and listened as the pastor read a sermon written by his grandfather. The pastor read the sermon and Eli could hear his grandfather's voice as he recounted his own sinful life and wonderful day of salvation. After telling about the wonderful experience of salvation and the "five greatest and most adventuresome years of my life," the pastor read the last paragraph.

"To all of you listening to this now, understand that I am not here. I am with my King fulfilling the greatest adventure in all eternity. The body you see lying in this casket is nothing more than the physical body of a spiritual being. I want you all to know that I love you dearly and I want nothing more than to see you all again in the presence of the Lord. The only way our reunion can take place is if you stop pushing God away and make a decision to place your faith in him. Please come and join me that we may share this adventure with our King together."

Eli knew that his grandfather penned those words with him in mind. He could feel the unmistakable tug of the Holy Spirit on his soul, and he knew what he had to do.

There isn't time now, Eli reasoned. *After the funeral. I promise, God, after the funeral.*

The funeral ended and after a short graveside service in the church's cemetery, there was a "celebration" reception for the family and friends at Eli's grandfather's house. At the reception, Eli's mother handed him a package with a note.

"He told me to give this to you, after the funeral," she said with tears rolling down her cheeks. "Dad loved you more than you can ever know. He always called you his favorite."

Eli thanked and hugged his mother, took the package, and went out the back door of the house. Eli knew where he was going and what he needed to do. Eli's grandfather owned several acres of land directly behind his house which Eli had spent many summer days exploring with his grandfather. Not too far from his grandfather's house on top of a hill was a large oak tree he and his grandfather used to sit under for hours. It was under this tree that they talked about everything. It was here that Eli told his grandfather everything, and it was here under this tree almost five years ago to the day that Eli sat and listened for hours as his grandfather talked and talked, cried and cried about his grandmother. Eli knew what he needed was to be found under the branches of this tree.

Eli walked away from the house until he thought he was not being watched and then ran toward the tree. The tree was not on the hill directly behind Eli's grandfather's house, but resided on a hill just on the other side of the hill closest the house. Eli and his grandfather liked this because when they went to the tree, they could not see any homes or businesses. Sitting under the tree made Eli feel that he was away from civilization as a whole.

Eli's heart was still racing as he slowed his pace and approached the tree. There on top of the hill overlooking the horizon was the old oak tree. The tree's massive branches soared into the air shading a large portion of lush green grass. Eli smiled as he noticed the large knot in the tree that looked like a door. His grandfather used to tell him when he was younger that the Keebler Elves lived in that tree and that was their doorway. Eli placed his hands on the familiar bark of the tree and inhaled a deep breath of the fresh familiar country air.

"Smells like heaven!" Eli said in the same way his grandfather always said it when they would come up to the tree.

After enjoying a few memories, and the incredible view of the surrounding landscape, Eli sat down and opened the note. Written in his grandfather's familiar handwriting, the note seemed more to Eli like an actual conversation with his grandfather than it did reading words on paper.

Dear Eli,

This feels really weird to write, but if you are reading this note, my time in the physical realm has already ended. If everything has gone according to plan, you will have already been to my funeral and heard the words I wrote to the family. As you probably guessed, I wrote those words with several of your uncles in mind, but mostly with you in mind. I messed up a lot as a father and as a result I have pushed away several of your uncles, but I have always felt that God has given me a chance to be a father again with you.

You are like a son to me, Eli, and as a son, I need to tell you that it is time that you stop playing around with God and make a choice to put your faith in Him. I know you better than you may think, and I know that when it comes to salvation that you know you are not saved. I know that you feel being a Christian has made my life dull and boring, but you cannot be more wrong.

Being a Christian is the most exciting thing that has ever happened to me. To be a child of the King is the most incredible adventure a being can ever know, and it is an adventure I want to share with you. Please, Eli, make a choice to call out to the King and then take the gifts I left for you and hold on to them. I have a feeling you will be needing them real soon. Until we meet again, may the Lord lead you and may His face shine upon you.

In the service of the King,
Grandpa

P.S. You were always my favorite

Eli laughed and cried at the same time. With tears rolling down his face, Eli opened the package. Inside he found his grandfather's old silver ring and a brand new Bible. This Bible was the exact same type of Bible his grandfather had. It had a blue cover with silver pages, which happened to be Eli's and his grandfather's favorite color combination. On the front of the Bible, Eli's name was engraved in sliver with a large silver sword engraved on the cover. Eli opened the Bible and sniffed the new smell as a small bookmark fell out of the Bible. It was one of the bookmark tracts his grandfather used to witness. It had the plan of salvation written on one side and the wordless book colors on the other. Eli held this bookmark in his hand and looked at the ring. The ring looked different than he remembered. It was silver with a large black center in the shape of a circle. But the black center, which was plain and empty, used to have the pictures of the Christian's armor, or at least Eli thought it did. Whatever the case, Eli did not want to waste any more time. He knew that he had not accepted Christ as his Savior, he knew that God was calling him to be saved right now, and he wanted to accept Christ not only because of his need for salvation but because he loved his grandfather and wanted to see him again.

Though Eli had grown up in church and thought he knew what the Bible taught about salvation, he chose to pick up the tract his grandfather left him and read over it. The tract was a simple one and recorded the Roman's Road. Eli read and he was reminded that the Bible teaches that everyone is a sinner in Romans 3:23. Further, Eli read that the payment for that sin is death, eternal separation from God forever, in Romans 6:23. The only way to escape that death is to accept the sacrifice of Jesus Christ as God's gift for salvation as taught in Romans 5:8 and Romans 6:23. The tract ended with an invitation to accept Jesus Christ and recorded Romans 10:9-13, which ended by claiming that anyone who calls on the name of Jesus will be saved.

Eli bowed his head and truly prayed for the first time. With the Word of God in his mind and the prompting of the Holy Spirit in his heart, Eli's prayer flowed smoothly out of his mouth.

"Dear God, thank You for today. Thank You for loving me and giving me another day of life. God, You know my heart; You know that I have rejected You for a long time. I know that You are God and that the Bible is true. I know that I am a sinner. I know I have done a lot of things that have hurt You and made You sad. I know that my sin's penalty is death and I know that there is nothing I can do to save myself. Lord Jesus, thank You for loving me and dying on the cross to pay for my sin. Thank You for being buried and rising again that I might live. Right now, God, I confess my sin! I am so sorry for my sin and for rejecting Your gift of salvation for so long! Please forgive me and save me. I believe in You and in what the Bible tells me about You. You tell us that if we believe in You, confess our sin, and call out to You that You will save us. Lord Jesus, I am calling out to You right now. Please save me and make me Yours. In Jesus' name I pray, amen."

As soon as Eli finished praying, he felt a sensation like nothing he had ever felt before. It was forgiveness, and something else. This must be what his grandfather talked about and called his "new life." Whatever it was, it was incredible! It was as if his body was filling with a warm liquid happiness. Eli sat back against the tree and closed his eyes.

"What a fool I have been for refusing salvation for so long! If this is the beginning, I cannot wait to see what Grandpa meant when he said the greatest adventure of all time awaits."

Eli laid against the tree with his legs sprawled out in front of him for several moments enjoying the freedom he felt in his soul. As the sun rose in the sky its warmth filled the air. Eli closed his eyes and fell asleep contemplating what his grandfather meant when he wrote that he hoped Eli would find the adventures his soul craved, not suspecting that he was about to find out.

chapter 4
a terrifying race

A bright flash of lightning followed by a boisterous rumble of thunder jolted Eli awake. It was now pitch black outside and the rain began falling in sheets.

Oh no! thought Eli. *I must have fallen asleep! Where did this storm come from?*

Eli stood up staring at the sky in wonder. The sky was black, not black like at night black, but pitch black, like the complete absence of color and light. Not only was the sky black, but it was void of anything but darkness. There were no clouds, no birds, and no light with the exception of the occasional lightning bolts. To make matters worse, Eli realized that though it was raining, his body was not getting wet. Curious, Eli looked down at his body and noticed that not only was his body somehow avoiding the rain, it was glowing! Further, his clothes seemed to have lost all their color and looked like they came from the old black-and-white movies his grandfather used to watch.

Another flash of lightning zoomed across the sky drawing Eli's attention up and onto the large oak tree.

Eli gasped. The branches of the tree and the luscious green leaves were dark black, and also seemed to have all the color sucked out of them. Eli examined the trunk of the tree and found the trunk looked more like a black outline of the tree. The tree's appearance reminded Eli of the time his art class at school developed pictures in a dark room. Eli felt as if he were staring at the negatives from a picture of the tree.

Eli stood perplexed for a moment, until another bright flash of lighting and crash of thunder told Eli that whatever the case with the tree, it was time for him to find shelter.

Eli tucked his Bible, note from his grandfather, and ring into his pants, and ran toward his grandfather's house.

Eli passed several more pitch black outlines of trees on his way toward the house, but that did not bother him as much as the glowing of his body. The glow from Eli's body seemed to pierce the darkness around him and illuminate his path as if Eli were carrying a flashlight—no, as if he was a flashlight.

Trying not to freak out, Eli decided to think about something else.

I wonder if my parents are worried about me? thought Eli. *No matter, I can't wait to tell them that I now know I am a Christian. I bet they will be so happy!*

Eli kept distracting himself from all the weird things around him as he ran up the final hill before his grandfather's house came into view. Eli topped the hill and stood in shock at what he saw. Instead of his grandfather's two-story, cape-cod style house, Eli saw what looked to be a stone castle complete with guard towers, battlements, a stone bridge, a mote, and iron gates! Unlike all of the trees, the sky, and all the grass around Eli, the castle was glowing with color. The color was not the only thing that made the castle stand out from its surroundings; inside the castle a warm yellow light filled all the windows. Further, on this side of the castle, darkness filled the sky and rain poured down, but on the other side of the castle were blue skies and warm sunshine as if the castle was a barrier that separated night from day.

"Okay," Eli said aloud. "Now I'm officially freaked out!"

The sunshine behind the castle provided an outline for Eli to see the massive size of the fortress. The castle, which looked a lot like the Tower of London Eli had to do a report on last year in school, was monstrous in comparison, being at least twice the size. All along the top of the outer walls were guard towers that jutted against the sunny background like massive hands from the ground.

Staring at the gigantic castle, standing where Eli's grandfather's house should have been, all the questions he had been pushing back since he woke up filled Eli's mind, making him feel like his mind would explode.

"What's going on? Why are all the trees black? Why is the rain avoiding me? Where did this castle come from? Where is my grandfather's house? Is it safe, should I go in there or should I go and try to find help? And why am I glowing?"

When Eli felt as though his mind could not be any more cluttered with questions, Eli's mind was forced to clear up in the most terrifying way possible. Out of the darkness came the most frightening voice Eli had ever heard.

"Elijah Storm!" yelled a growling voice followed by a sinister, blood curdling laugh. "I have been waiting for you!"

As the creature yelled the last syllable, Eli could tell by the inflection in its voice that it began running towards him. Only one thought filled Eli's mind.

I have to get to that castle, fast!

Eli launched into a mad sprint to the castle. Though he was one of the fastest kids in his class, Eli did not like his chances of making it to the castle before the creature caught up to him.

For one, Eli thought, *the ground is rough and rocky, and the rain is making it slippery. And for another thing,* bemoaned Eli, *that thing sounded large and scary so naturally it is probably also very fast.*

Eli was still about fifty yards from the castle when he heard another bloodthirsty laugh, this time much closer than before. Startled, Eli screamed at the castle, "Help! Help! Someone help me! There is something out here and it is trying to get me! Someone please help me!"

Immediately Eli could decipher movement inside the castle and hear the rush of excited voices calling out to one another. Hope sprung up in Eli's heart that he might actually make it to safety, when he heard a noise that chased all hope away. Large, heavy, padded footsteps splashing in the water approaching fast. As the steps grew closer, Eli heard the panting of a massive set of lungs drawing near, ready to strike its prey. Eli's mind tried to plan an evasion route when the loud bloodthirsty voice roared a deafening roar directly behind him.

Two things happened simultaneously: Eli's body locked up and he tumbled headlong into the grass in front of him, and the iron gates on the castle walls flung open.

Light exploded from the open gates, flooding the darkness and reaching Eli just as he felt the warm breath of whatever was chasing him on his back as he tumbled. Eli heard the creature roar in pain and heard the sound of large paws retreating into the darkness. Eli had just enough time to look behind him to see what looked like the back end and the tail of a massive lion-like creature descending back into the darkness.

Petrified, Eli lay motionless in the wet grass as the raindrops avoided his body. Though he heard the sound of wings and the voices of men calling out to him, all Eli could think about was how close he had come to being devoured by the creature. The sound of wings and the voices of the men quickly reached Eli's location and several hands grabbed him under his arms and dragged him in the direction of the castle. Startled, Eli yelled and flung himself onto his own feet.

"What was that thing?" Eli exclaimed. "I mean what was that—" Eli's voice trailed off as he looked at his rescuers.

In the light cast from the gate of the castle, Eli caught the first glimpse of his rescuers—a group of three armored soldiers who resembled cherubs. The men were short and muscular with breastplates, helmets, and swords drawn ready for a fight. In the middle of their backs were two feathery wings flapping in a slow rhythm allowing the creatures to hover in place. Overall, Eli thought they looked like cupids on steroids.

"Who are you? What are you? Where am I?" sputtered Eli.

"Calm down, son," one soldier said as he looked intently into the darkness. "We will have time to answer your questions after we get you inside."

"Yes, come Elijah. The Enemy does not like the light, but he is not one for giving up easily," spoke another cherub as he returned his sword to its sheaf and gently placed a hand on Eli's shoulder.

Shocked at the fact that the cherub guy knew his name, Eli simply nodded his head and followed the lead cherub, the one who placed his hand on Eli's shoulder. With the two other cherubs flying backward facing the darkness with weapons drawn, the group resembled a triangle with Eli in the middle as they briskly walked and flew back to the castle gate. Though Eli was far from trusting when it came to his rescuers, Eli knew that at least he would be safe from the lion creature and of the two, the cherubs seemed far more favorable.

Eli followed the three soldiers through the large outer gates of the walls and immediately the gates closed and locked behind them. Upon entering the castle yard that spanned from the gates to the keep, Eli heard the noise of excitement and voices ring down from the windows throughout the large fortress. The group traveled toward the keep and approached two large golden doors that stood at least fifteen feet high and ten feet wide. When the lead cherub pointed at the doors, the doors opened upon command.

"In there, Master Storm. You will be safe in there," said the lead cherub.

Again feeling the shock that these creatures knew his name, Eli walked through the doors and stood as the large golden doors closed when the lead cherub pointed at them. The doors closed and Eli was sure of two things: the lion creature could not enter the castle and Eli could not leave the castle.

chapter 5
of friends and enemies

Try as he might to keep his guard up and not gain a sense of false security, Eli could not help but be mesmerized by the castle. Before he realized what he was doing, Eli found himself turning in a circle with his mouth gaping open in awe at his surroundings.

Eli had never seen such magnificence. Inside the stone castle was a radiant light that not only illuminated everything in a spectacular way, but somehow gave Eli a sense of peace and comfort as well. Where this light came from, Eli had no idea. He did not see one chandelier, one lamp, not even one candle, and yet the whole castle was as bright as a summer's day.

The light was amazing but so was what the light illuminated. The floors of the castle were made of what looked like pure white marble gorgeously accented with glittering gold and black swirls. Eli had no idea how the floors were made because there were no seams or cracks; it was as if the floors were made out of one ridiculously large piece of marble. The walls of the castle were made out of the same marble material only they were the opposite colors—a solid black marble with glittering white and gold accents—and also seemed to be cut from one solid piece of marble. The only breaks in the walls were large arched doorways flanked by two white marble pillars. There were four doorways in this entry room, the entrance Eli walked through, a door directly in front of him on the far side of the room and a door in the middle of the walls on either side of Eli. Eli could not see how tall the walls were but he could see large golden banners with a crimson cross in the center of them hanging from the beams of the ceiling. All over the walls were extravagant large portraits of men and women wearing armor inside gorgeous golden frames. Eli's eyes looked all around the room and then came to a stop looking at the three soldiers who were staring back at him.

Seeing the three men shook Eli out of his temporary hypnotic state. The three men, no taller than four feet yet all with the chiseled appearance of grown men, looked nearly identical except for their eye, wing, and hair color. After a few awkward moments, one of the men who had bright orange coloring for his eyes, wings, and hair, who also happened to be the lead cherub, introduced himself.

"I am Zephyr, servant of the Great King," said the cherub as he took off his helmet and bowed hovering in the air.

Zephyr's voice was calming to Eli and somehow Eli could not shake the feeling that he knew Zephyr and that they were friends.

Then came the second who had a deep blue coloring.

"I am Ike, servant of the Great King," said the cherub as he also bowed and removed his helmet.

The third man approached and as he did he took off his helmet to reveal fire-engine red hair and eyes to go with his fire-engine red wings.

"I am Brutus, servant of the Great King," said the cherub in a grizzled voice that reminded Eli of his football coach.

Eli noticed that the three cherubs were looking at him and he felt the need to introduce himself. "I-I-I am..."

"Elijah," interrupted Zephyr. "Elijah Storm."

"We know who you are, and we've been waiting for you," Brutus cut in. "From the looks of it, we were not the only ones either."

"How do you know who I am, and how did you know I was going to be here? And can anyone tell me what that thing was out there and how that thing knew I was going to be here?"

Zephyr turned and said something to Ike, the blue-colored one, and Ike flew off through one of the large doorways. As Zephyr turned and faced Eli again, Brutus asked, "Are you not the grandson of David Granite, the Master Defender?"

"The what?" replied Eli as he squinted his eyes and tilted his head.

"The Master Defender," replied Brutus, speaking a little slower this time, as if the only reason Eli did not understand what he was talking about was an inability to properly hear Brutus.

"Brutus," Zephyr cut in. "Perhaps we should stick with what this young man would be familiar with. Remember, this is the first time Elijah has graced our presence."

"You're right," Brutus replied. "Is David Granite your grandfather?"

"Yes he *was*, but how do you, I mean, how did you know him?"

Zephyr hovered close to Eli and again Eli could swear he had met Zephyr somewhere before.

"Your grandfather told us you would be coming. We are friends of your grandfather and we are your friends as well. You won't understand what I am about to tell you, but your grandfather is one of the greatest defenders this realm has ever known. I will explain more when it is appropriate, but for now, I want to assure you that you are out of danger and in the company of friends. Follow us and we will lead you to your room. There you will find some new clothes, food, and a note your grandfather left for you."

Distracted a little by the strange familiarity he felt toward Zephyr, Eli replied, "You mean my grandfather *was* one of the greatest defenders. I hate to tell you this but my grandfather is dead."

Zephyr raised his eyebrows and looked as if he were going to respond to Eli's statement when Ike returned.

"All is ready for Master Storm," he announced. He flew to the side of the doorway he returned from and motioned with his left hand for the group to walk through the door.

"Wonderful! Well, shall we be off?" asked Zephyr as he looked at Eli expectantly.

"Sure," said Eli as he walked toward the door on the far wall in front of him.

Ike led them down the hallway filled with doors to other rooms. One such room Eli stopped to look into was filled with the most luxurious furniture Eli had ever seen, all surrounding a buffet table that nearly spanned the entire width of the room.

"This is the room of fellowship," said Ike, who had noticed Eli's interest in the room. "You will find few gatherings in all creation that can rival a room full of the King's servants fellowshipping and celebrating the goodness of the King with each other."

"Especially if the food is good," added Brutus as the cherubs laughed.

The company continued down the hallway and Eli could not help but look into each room as he passed by. In every room there were more large portraits of men and women in armor, more cherubs, and more golden banners.

"Who are the people in the paintings?" asked Eli.

"They are defenders who serve the King," replied Zephyr. "The King honors the defenders by giving them a portrait among other things. Your grandfather has a portrait currently hanging in the war room. If all goes according to plan, you will have the opportunity to see it."

"Okay," said Eli, as he really did not know how to process that his grandfather could be a hero and have a giant portrait hanging somewhere in this place.

"So what was that thing that was chasing me?" asked Eli as they continued down the hall.

"That was the Enemy of the Great King," said Zephyr as he and Brutus exchanged a pained look.

"Enemy?" questioned Eli. "If the King is so great, how can He have an enemy?"

Zephyr's face turned somber. "Many years ago the Enemy served the Great King as one of the King's most trusted and elevated servants. The King loved the Enemy and gave him a position and beauty of great elevation."

"So what happened?" prodded Eli when it seemed Zephyr had finished his explanation.

"Well, Master Storm, one day, the Enemy lifted his heart up against the King and desired to be King. The Enemy rebelled against the King and with him one third of the entire King's servants."

"No way!" exclaimed Eli. "What happened then?"

"The King banished the Enemy and all the rebellious servants and condemned them to eternal punishment and doom. One day the King will gather up all the wicked servants as well as the Enemy and execute their punishment. Until that day, the King allows the Enemy and all his minions to roam the realms."

"What does the Enemy want with me?"

"The Enemy has no power to harm the King directly. The only way the Enemy can hinder the work of the King is by attempting to destroy the King's servants before they are able to be used and empowered by the King. The King's Word describes the actions of the Enemy: 'As a roaring lion seeking whom he may devour.' The Enemy knew that once you reached the light of the castle, you would be out of his reach. He was attempting to devour you before you could become a defender for the King."

"Are you telling me the Enemy was going to eat me?" asked Eli in shock.

"For lack of a better explanation, yes," replied Zephyr.

The hallway spilled out into a large room with several staircases. To Eli's amazement, the staircases were made of what looked like pure gold.

"Your room is up the right set of stairs and is the third door on the left. Is there anything else you need?" asked Ike.

Before Eli could respond, Zephyr replied, "Thank you Ike; that is enough. We will escort Master Storm from here. Thank you again for your support in going out and retrieving him. I know that sort of thing is not what you are used to."

Ike smiled and bowed. "It was my pleasure. It is not every day that one has the opportunity to rescue a long awaited Predestine."

With that, Ike smiled at Eli and flew back down the hallway from which the company had just come.

Looking confused, Eli turned toward Zephyr. "What did he mean by, 'Predestine'?"

"Tomorrow, Eli," said Zephyr, "we will have time to discuss all of your questions after you have had time to rest, eat, and read the letter your grandfather left for you."

The company of three ascended the right staircase and stopped in front of the third door on the left. Eli stood and looked at the door in amazement. The door had "Predestine Elijah Storm" engraved on a golden name plate at eye level in the center of the door.

"Can I please just ask you one more question?" asked Eli quietly and calmly though he thought he was going to explode on the inside.

"If you think it will help," said Brutus as he looked over at Zephyr as if to say, "Why won't he just go in the room?"

"Okay," said Eli as he took a deep breath, trying to stay calm. "Could you please tell me how my grandfather was this incredible hero when he never left our town for any amount of time? I mean, my grandpa never traveled, never missed a weekend at the nursing home, and was never gone! How could he have been a 'Master Defender' and how could he have known that I would be coming here?"

"That is a good question, or questions I should say," said Brutus in a gentle tone. "But we said you could ask a question; we never promised you we would answer your question."

Brutus and Zephyr chuckled as Eli gave them both an amused look.

"You have had a long night," continued Brutus. "I suggest you go into your room, change clothes, eat some food, and read the letter your grandfather left for you. I am positive that what you read in the letter will set the groundwork for us to be able to answer the rest of your questions. I am sure it is frustrating, but all your questions simply cannot be answered on your first night here."

Too exhausted to argue, Eli conceded and Zephyr opened the door. Smiling at what was being called his room, all Eli could say was, "No way!"

chapter 6
a new adventure

"This is my room?" asked Eli in a mixture of a question and exclamation. "Like my room, my room?"

Zephyr nodded. "Yes, this is your room."

"Wow!" said Eli trying to calm down a little. "I think I could get used to this place."

As with all the rooms in this castle, Eli's room was massive. The same combination of marble covered his floors and his walls but the floor of his room had several large fur rugs. The room was rectangular in shape with the wall opposite the door completely made up of gigantic floor-to-ceiling windows and two large French doors in the center of the wall leading to a balcony. Covering all of the windows were floor-to-ceiling thick velvet golden drapes. The drapes hung from solid gold rods and had red-colored ropes which could be used to draw the drapes open. Behind the drapes, a flood of warm light filled the outside of the castle. Eli realized that his room must face the other side of the castle rather than the side with all of the rain and darkness.

The wall with the door located on it was plain in comparison to the magnificent wall of windows, but did boast a giant fireplace in the center of the room. About ten feet out from the fireplace and located in the center of the large fur rug was an extravagant work desk with ornate carvings. A luscious throne-like chair with golden outline and crimson padding sat directly behind the desk. On the far side of the room was the largest four-poster bed Eli had ever seen. The comforter on the bed was deep crimson and the pillows were covered with golden silk pillow cases. On the right side of the room, covering a large portion of the massive marble wall, were several gigantic flat screens that Eli assumed must be the largest televisions he had ever seen in his life. Facing the wall of screens was a beautiful, plush, leather sectional complete with a built-in mini-fridge and cup holders.

"Now this is a room!" exclaimed Eli.

"Wonderful, so you approve of it then?" asked Zephyr.

"Approve, of course I approve," replied Eli. "I mean, you know it is not what I am used to but it's not bad."

Eli smiled at Zephyr to make sure he understood that he was joking.

"Well, maybe next time we can do better." Zephyr laughed as he ushered Eli into the room.

Walking through the room, Eli noticed an envelope on the desk with his name written in golden ink in his grandfather's handwriting.

"That," said Zephyr, pointing to the letter, "is the letter your grandfather left for you. And those are new clothes for you to put on." Zephyr pointed to some clothes lying on the bed.

"Ike has already ordered some food to be brought to you. It will be here shortly. I suggest you change your clothes, eat some food, and sit down to read your letter. I know you are confused and scared, but trust me; things will be different in the morning. Until then, I wish you a good night."

"Night?" questioned Eli. "How can it be night? It is a beautiful sunny day outside."

"Of course it is," said Zephyr in a matter of fact way. "It is always bright and shining in the kingdom of the Great King."

Zephyr made his way out of the room where Brutus was waiting for him.

"Oh, okay, thank you," shouted Eli as the door closed behind them.

Eli walked over to the bed and examined the clothes laid out for him. Eli thought the clothes resembled the outfits athletes wear during the Olympics. The outfit consisted of several layers. The first layer was made up of a brilliantly pure white material that Eli had never seen before. The material looked like Eli's elastic dry-wear that he wore to exercise, only it was a radiant sparkling white color and it felt as soft as a baby-blanket. There was a long-sleeved shirt in this material, as well as a pair of pants that stretched all the way down to Eli's ankles. To go on top of that layer was a brilliant blue sleeveless shirt made of the same elastic dry-wear material. The front of the sleeveless shirt had a four-inch wide sparkling metallic silver stripe running from the right shoulder down to the left hip. On the left breast of the tunic was a small metallic silver cross. Lying on the bed next to the clothes was a three-inch-wide silver belt made out of a plastic-like material with a shiny brilliant blue buckle in the shape of a shield and what looked like a sheaf on the left side of the buckle. Next to the belt was a pair of silver athletic shoes also made out of the plastic-like material.

Eli took off his colorless clothes and replaced them with the clothes from the bed. Not only were the clothes soft, they also felt warm to Eli's skin as if they had just come out of the dryer on a cold morning. The moment the outfit was complete, the clothes began to hum with energy and light radiated from them. The light grew brighter and brighter until Eli could not see his clothes for the brightness of the light. In an instant, the light faded away and Eli marveled at his clothes. The clothes seemed to have bonded with his skin, creating a body armor that was flexible and comfortable. Eli could see the armor as if he was wearing normal clothes, and yet they provided no discomfort or restrictions on his movements.

This is awesome! Eli tested the new clothes by doing a series of stretches and exercises. *I wish I had a set of these back home!*

Eli's thoughts were interrupted by a loud knock on his door.

"Come in," called Eli as he stood up from doing push-ups.

The door opened to reveal another cherub, with a purple coloring for the eyes, wings, and hair, holding a covered silver platter.

"Dinner, for Predestine Elijah Storm," announced the cherub in a startling deep voice.

"Thank you," said Eli as he walked over and accepted the platter.

The cherub bowed and then flew out of the room shutting the door behind him. Eli took the platter over to the desk and set the platter down next to the note from his grandfather.

Deciding to eat before he opened the note from his grandfather, Eli opened the platter, which contained an assortment of different colored foods the likes of which Eli had never seen. There was a bright yellow fruit that looked like a carrot yet had the texture of Jell-O, a fluorescent pink cluster of what looked like grapes, and a pink cotton-candy textured mini-loaf of bread. Along with all of the food was a solid gold goblet full of sparkling clear water.

Eli ate until he was full, and to Eli's amazement, everything tasted great. Eli picked up the goblet and emptied the refreshingly cool water with several large gulps. Satisfied, Eli picked up the envelope containing his grandfather's note and collapsed onto the bed.

Alright, Grandpa, Eli thought. *I can't wait to hear what you have to say about all of this!*

Eli examined the envelope as he turned it over in his hand to open it. The paper was a thick parchment and it was sealed with a deep red wax with a cross stamped on the seal. Eli broke the seal and took out the letter. All of the lettering sparkled in the light of the room as if his grandfather used golden ink to write with, making it easy for Eli to read.

Dear Elijah,

I want to begin by telling you that I love you and I am proud of you for taking the steps to be where you are right now. I am sure you are wondering where you are and why you are here. You are in the spirit realm. This is the supernatural side of the world your physical body lives in. In making your journey here, you have accepted Jesus Christ as your Savior. When you did that, you felt a thrilling sensation fill your body. That was the awakening of your spirit. This is the world in which your spirit dwells. I wish I could explain it better, but I am sure you will be able to get a more detailed explanation from one of the Angelos you met upon your arrival.

Speaking of which, the people you have met that probably remind you of cherubs are called Angelos, but you know them better as angels. The Angelos peoples are the ministers of the Great King, the Triune-God of the King's Word. You know Him best as Jehovah, Jesus, and the Holy Ghost. The Angelos were created to minister to the King and to human beings through the commandments of the King. They are not your enemies; in fact, you will find through your time in this realm, that they are some of your closest allies and friends.

The reason why you are here is because I want you to take my place as defender of this realm. Since the time of my salvation, I have had the privilege of serving the King and fighting the Enemy. I have been informed that my time in this capacity is coming to a close. I must move on to serve the King in another role. To fulfill this role, my spirit is to leave the physical realm that I may serve the King full-time in the spirit realm. Now that I must move on, the peoples of this realm need a new person who will take up the call and serve the King. Elijah, I can't think of anyone I would want to follow in my footsteps more than you!

I know what you must be thinking, but no, you are not dreaming. I remember the first time I found myself where you are right now, I thought for sure I had blown a gasket and would soon be in a loony bin! This is not a dream; this is more real than anything you have known up to this point in your life. Tomorrow, you will be presented with a choice to accept your calling from the King, begin your mission training, and follow in my footsteps or reject it and return to the physical realm. Your calling is to complete your training for the King, find your identity as a defender, and fight the Enemy and his minions.

This calling is truly an incredible honor; however, it comes with great difficulty. Before you look at the difficulty, understand one thing, son. The King who desires your service is the same King who chose to purchase you from the Enemy by spilling His own blood. The Great King paid a price that included far more pain and sorrow than you can imagine ransoming your soul. Yes, I'm talking about Jesus and His sacrifice. Now, He seeks your allegiance and service.

The road is not an easy one, but I know that you have too much of your old grandpa in you to turn down an incredible adventure. I love you Elijah, more than I could ever express. There are so many things I want to write in *this letter, but you would not understand. Don't fret, this is not the last time you will hear from me. I will leave you now and let you think about the choice you must make.*

Forever in the service of the King,
Grandpa

Eli read the letter several times wishing it did not end. It felt as if his grandfather was in the room with him as he read, and Eli did not want to let go of that feeling.

Thinking about everything his grandfather wrote to him, Eli lay down on the bed and covered himself with the sheets and comforter.

"I don't know why the King would want me to follow in your footsteps, Grandpa, but if He really does want to use me then I would be honored to serve Him."

Eli did not understand why, but every time someone mentioned the "King" or referenced the "King's Word" in any way, his insides burned with excitement. Even though Eli had just been saved earlier that day, he felt a strong love and loyalty toward the King.

Though he did not know what the morning would bring, Eli new that this was the start of something great. Eli thought he was too excited to sleep, but as he lay on the silky sheets he felt the exhaustion of the day overcome him. As he closed his eyes, he smiled, welcoming the sleep and the promise of a new adventure.

chapter 7
the chosen one

A flood of light sweeping over Eli awoke him from his slumber. One by one, the drapes that covered the wall of windows were opening, allowing the warm energizing light from outside into the room. Basking in the warmth of the light, Eli stretched and enjoyed the feeling of the cool silky sheets. Eli got out of the bed and evaluated the situation.

It wasn't a dream after all, mused Eli as he examined his clothes that seemed to have morphed with his body. *So I really am in the spirit realm. Cool.*

A soft knock on the door sounded through the room.

"Come in," called Eli.

The door opened and Zephyr and Brutus flew into the room.

"Good morning, Predestine Storm!" they spoke in unison.

"Good morning," replied Eli, smiling at their enthusiasm.

"How did you sleep?" asked Zephyr curiously. "How are you feeling today now that you have read your grandfather's note and have rested?"

"I am still feeling a little surreal," answered Eli. "But all in all, I am excited about what all this might mean."

"Wonderful to hear," said Brutus. "I see your new armor fits you well. How do you like it?"

"Armor?" asked Eli. "Oh, yeah, the clothes. I like them a lot! They are really cool. But, if you don't mind me asking, what happened to my old clothes?" asked Eli as he noticed they were not where he had left them the night before.

"We had them disposed of," replied Zephyr.

"Disposed of? What do you mean, you had my clothes disposed of?"

"Don't worry about it," cut in Brutus. "You are in the spirit realm now; those clothes are from the physical realm and will not do you any good here. When you return to the physical realm you will find your clothes still on your physical body. Oh, and by the way, Ike said they found these in your clothes." Brutus produced a bag containing Eli's grandfather's ring, note, and the Bible Eli received after the funeral.

"Thanks," said Eli as he took the objects.

Eli placed the ring on his right hand ring finger and the note in the Bible, but could not find a place for the Bible.

"Your belt has a place to sheave your Bible," Zephyr cut in as he realized Eli's quandary. "Just there on your left hip."

"Oh yeah," said Eli as he remembered seeing the sheaf when he put the belt on.

The Bible fit in the sheaf as if the sheaf were custom made for the Bible. It was then that Eli realized his armor matched his Bible. Eli looked up at the Angelos.

"Is it a coincidence that my armor and my Bible match?"

"No," replied Zephyr. "You will find that there are no coincidences here in the spirit realm. You have always favored Bibles with the blue and silver coloring, have you not?"

"Yes," answered Eli.

"That desire has nothing to do with anything from your physical body, but everything to do with your spiritual body. Though I don't fully understand why humans are prone to certain color combinations, you will find that your preferences in life are intertwined with who you are in this realm."

"Cool," was the only answer Eli could muster.

Eli thought about all the different preferences he had in life, wondering which ones would translate into the spiritual realm. Before Eli could ask a question about pumpkin pie, his favorite dessert, Brutus added, "If you think your armor and Bible are cool, just wait until you see what happens to Zephyr when—"

Before Brutus could finish, Zephyr waved his hand. "Let's not get ahead of ourselves, Brutus. There is too much that we need to accomplish now for us to be looking too far into the future."

"You're right; I apologize," said Brutus looking sheepish.

"Wait," cut in Eli. "What was he about to say?"

"Brutus was going to reference something that might or might not happen depending upon choices that must be made shortly."

"Choices?" said Eli. "What kind of choices? Who is making these choices?"

"Why, you are, Master Storm," said Brutus with a look toward Zephyr like he was trying to redeem himself. "But you will not make these choices just yet. You will get there soon enough. Until then, Zephyr is right, we have much to accomplish in the present."

Following that statement, the two Angelos flew out the door motioning for Eli to follow.

"My grandfather's letter explained that I am in the spirit realm and a little bit about what that means, but I had a few questions I was hoping you could answer for me," began Eli as the group descended the golden staircase.

"I'm sure we can." Brutus smiled. "Fire away, Master Storm."

"Well, if I am in the spirit realm, does that mean that I have died in the physical realm?"

"No, you have not passed from your physical life. You are still very much alive in the physical realm. In fact, one of the main qualities that separate a defender from some of the other positions in the King's army is the fact that the defender has both a physical and spiritual life," replied Zephyr as they walked down the stairs and into the hallway from the night before.

"Then where is my body? Is it okay? Do you have someone watching over it to make sure animals don't get it or anything?"

The Angelos smiled as Brutus answered, "Your body is fine. All the time you spend here in this realm will amount to less than an instant in the physical realm. When you return to the physical realm, you will be returned to your body the exact instant you transferred from the physical realm to the spirit realm."

"So that is how Grandpa was able to be a defender in this realm without us ever noticing him being gone. By the way, what did my grandpa do that made him so great here?"

"I wish we could tell you everything," said Zephyr as he led the group through a doorway that Eli had never been through before. "But most of it would not make sense to you just yet. What you can understand about your grandfather is that for the past five thousand years, your grandfather served the King to the best of his ability with a zeal, passion, and love for the King that was rare even for defenders. Your grandfather was faithful to the King both in this realm and in the physical realm and the King rewarded his faithfulness with great victories."

"Hold on!" exclaimed Eli. "You said five thousand years. What do you mean my grandfather served the King for the past five thousand years? My grandfather was only saved for about five years."

"The spiritual realm and the physical realm do not run on the same time frame. The King created time and is therefore not bound by time. Time is something the King created to dictate the physical realm not the spirit realm. A few moments here can equal many years in your realm and many years here can also equal only a few moments in your realm. It all depends on the commandment of the King. As it pertains to your grandfather's time of service, the King saw fit to allow your grandfather's time of service to extend through five thousand spirit realm years."

"That's right," added Brutus. "That is one reason why the King chose to promote your grandfather to the spirit realm full-time. Your grandfather's consistent faithfulness is one reason why your grandfather is still having an impact all throughout our realm."

Eli froze in place, not able to take another step. "Did you just say that my grandfather is still having an impact, as if he is still alive?" asked Eli.

"Of course he is," answered Brutus. "Remember it is only the physical body that is temporary. Your soul lives for eternity."

Eli was so excited that he could barely contain himself in order to ask his next question. "So does that mean I can see him again?"

Before Brutus could respond, Zephyr cut in, "I will answer that question; thank you, Brutus. The simple answer to your question is yes."

Eli's world instantly erupted into a barrage of thoughts and questions. Overcome with this new hope and realization, Eli opened his mouth but was silenced by Zephyr motioning with his hand for Eli to listen.

"Eli, your grandfather is alive and well here in the spirit realm and he is serving the King with all the passion and faithfulness that he had when you knew him in the physical realm. But he is honoring the King right now and only the King can give him leave to see you. Right now the King desires you to focus on Him, not your grandfather. You have choices to make and you have to decide what you will do with the life the King has given you. It is best if you do not get sidetracked with the possibility of all the wonderful blessings in the spirit realm."

"I understand," said Eli, a little deflated. "Can I ask you one more question then I promise I will be done for now?"

"Sure." Brutus laughed. "But something tells me this will not be your last question."

"So, forgive me if this sounds weird," began Eli a little sheepishly. "But am I still me? I mean, if I am separated from my body, am I missing anything or am I completely intact? Like, is this real or like a dream?"

"That is a fair question, Eli," replied Brutus as the three stopped outside a doorway with two frosted crystal doors radiating with light from the inside. "The King created all humans with both a physical life and spirit life. Your spirit life is what the King's Word calls your soul. Your soul is what gives your physical body life. You are you, because the real life inside your physical body is your soul. Think of your physical body as a house. You live in your house and your life gives your house life. Your house does not give your body life. Your soul is what gives your body life; your body is just the physical realm house for your soul. As for this being real, the spirit realm is very real, and everything you experience is also real."

At that moment, the doors swung open toward the group and Ike flew out of the doors.

"Everything is ready for the Predestine," announced Ike as he bowed in the air and motioned with his left arm for the group to proceed through the doors.

"Thank you very much, Ike," said Zephyr. "May the King honor your faithfulness. Come this way Elijah, and perhaps we can speak more as we dine."

The group entered the room and Ike flew in front of them and proclaimed, "May I present to you the dining hall of the Son!"

Eli thought that this dining hall must be the most beautiful room ever built. The room was medium sized and completely round. Three of the four walls were made out of seamless frosted crystal that allowed the warm and energizing light to engulf the room. The only wall not made of the frosted crystal was the wall that connected the room to the castle and that wall looked as if it were covered in solid gold. The ceiling of the room was divided into five triangular sections of brilliant colors, each sectioned off with golden borders with the skinny part of the triangle facing the center of the room. There was a deep emerald green, a radiant ruby red, a rich sapphire blue, a stunning topaz, and a brilliant diamond. Each of these sections looked like they were made up of a single gigantic precious stone. What made the room absolutely amazing was the fact that the ceiling of precious stones was slowly rotating clockwise producing a gorgeous kaleidoscope feeling to the room.

Ike motioned the group to a table that stood in the center of the room. With all of the extravagance, the table seemed out of place. The table looked ancient and not all that well constructed. The closer Eli came to the table, he realized that etched into the table were several lines of words inlayed with gold. When Eli arrived at the table, he stooped over to read what the words said.

And as they were eating, Jesus took bread, blessed and broke it, and gave it to the disciples and said, "Take, eat; this is My body." Then He took the cup, and gave thanks, and gave it to them, saying, "Drink from it, all of you. For this is My blood of the new covenant, which is shed for many for the remission of sins. But I say to you, I will not drink of this fruit of the vine from now on until that day when I drink it new with you in My Father's kingdom."

Matthew 26:26-29

"Ah, yes," said Zephyr as he hovered next to Eli. "The last supper of the Lord."

"Yeah," said Eli. "I know the story, but why is it carved on this table?"

"Because this is *the* table from the last supper!"

"No way!" exclaimed Eli. "How is that possible?"

Brutus laughed a mischievous laugh. "Well, we knew such a monumental event should never be forgotten, and so a few of us sought permission to claim this earthly table and transport it to the spirit realm."

"You stole the table from the last supper?" accused a highly amused Eli.

"No, no, no!" cut in Zephyr. "We did not steal anything. We traded tables. And don't look at us like that; we gave the owner of that room a much finer table than we took! You could say we did that man a favor!"

Eli, Brutus, and Zephyr all burst into laughter before Ike gently insisted that they sit in the three chairs with their nameplates on them. Zephyr's nameplate and Brutus' nameplate rested on the two outside chairs while a third nameplate for "The Predestine" rested on the chair in the middle.

Eli was about to ask Zephyr about the repeating of the name "Predestine" when an Angelos with neon green coloring for his eyes, wings, and hair approached the table. With a swipe of his hand, the new Angelos produced golden plates and silverware and pure white napkins at each of the place settings. With a satisfied smile, the Angelos then snapped and produced more exotic fruit on the three plates.

"Enjoy your food, Predestine," said the Angelos as he bowed.

"Thank you, Murray," spoke Zephyr. "As always you honor the King with your faithfulness."

Smiling and bowing, the neon green-colored Angelos flew out of the door.

Eli recognized some of the fruit on his plate as some of the same fruit he ate the previous night. There were a few exceptions like the solid gold-colored pear, and bananas with rainbow-colored peels and insides. As was the case the previous night, Eli found every bite of fruit to be pleasing. Throughout the meal, a stream of Angelos of all different colors came through the room smiling and bowing to Eli. Several of these Angelos also greeted Eli with different phrases such as, "The King's face shine on you, Predestine," and, "The King bless you, Predestine."

Full and curious, Eli leaned over to Zephyr. "Hey Zephyr."

"Yes, Master Storm."

"Do you mind if I call you Zeph?"

"Not at all."

"Cool, thanks. Why is everyone looking at me like that, and why are they calling me the 'Predestine'?"

Zephyr smiled. "Predestine means 'the chosen one,' and they call you that and are eager to see you because we have been awaiting your arrival for many years."

"You've been waiting on me for many years?" Eli responded. "How can that be? My grandfather only passed away a few days ago. Wait, never mind," said Eli, remembering their previous conversation. "You said that time is not the same here. So I am guessing that the past few days in the physical realm has equaled what...two or three thousand years here."

"Exactly. Well not exactly," replied Zephyr with an amused look on his face. "The past few days since the physical passing of your grandfather has equaled right at one thousand years here. I know it is difficult but give it some time and you will begin to understand the different workings of each realm."

"Now, when you say 'give it some time,'" said Eli with a smile on his face, "are you talking about time as in physical realm time or time as in spiritual realm time? Because I don't know if I am up for being in school for another thousand years."

"That all depends on you and how well you pay attention," quipped Zephyr. "Enough about time, getting back to you being the Predestine. As I said, Predestine means 'the chosen one,' and every potential defender is given that title when they receive the call from the King. Our realm has been eagerly awaiting the next defender whom the King would bring to aid in our battle against the Enemy. Since the promotion of your grandfather, the Enemy has been very active in warring against the King, especially in our region. But now you have arrived and your arrival has sent a jolt of excitement all throughout the spirit realm and in our region in particular. The news of the arrival of the chosen one to fight for the King has ignited much excitement."

A wave of nausea hit Eli and he felt like he was going to be sick. *Chosen one,* Eli thought to himself. *How can I be the chosen one?*

Breakfast ended and their plates were whisked away by Murray. Ike returned and ushered Brutus, Zephyr, and Eli out of the room and led the group down the corridors. Eli, still stunned by what he had heard, walked in silence through the great halls of portraits. Noticing Eli's somber mood, Zephyr asked, "Is everything okay, Eli?"

Eli stopped walking and bowed his head in shame.

"Guys," Eli started, trying not to look at them. "I think there has been a mistake. I am not the chosen one; I can't be the chosen one you have waited for. I am not a good Christian in the other realm; in fact, I have rejected the invitation of the King for a long time before I decided to put my faith in Jesus. To be honest with you guys, I am probably the last person in the world who you would ever want to be the chosen one."

Eli continued to look down, tracing the black and gold swirls in the white marble, waiting to hear a condemnation from the Angelos. Instead of condemnation or panic, Brutus flew back from Eli a little as if he were an artist getting a better look at a canvas.

"Did you hear that, Zephyr?" Brutus asked loudly.

"I sure did," answered Zephyr in a somber tone.

"Do you know who he sounds like?" continued Brutus with a smile widening on his face.

"Absolutely!" replied Zephyr, as he too was smiling so wide that he looked to be on the brink of laughter.

A little confused as to what the Angelos found funny, Eli looked up and asked, "What's so funny? I thought you would be upset. Who do I sound like?"

"Son," answered Brutus, "you sound exactly like your grandfather did when we told him why we were calling him the Predestine. In fact it was right about this spot that your grandfather stopped walking and argued with us about who he was for almost an hour!"

"I remember that," said Zephyr. "Poor Krane nearly hit your grandfather on the head and dragged him to the general!"

"Wait," said Eli. "Who is this Krane?"

"Krane was your grandfather's guardian Angelos, and was afraid that after all the time spent on reaching your grandfather that he was going to lose him before he made it to the general," answered Brutus.

"What do you mean, 'guardian Angelos'? Are you saying that every human has an Angelos assigned to him? So what, I guess one of you is my guardian? Wait! Is this the reason why I feel like I know you, Zeph? Does this have something to do with what you said earlier about something being cool about Zephyr and my Bible?"

"Hold it right there," commanded Zephyr. "As I said earlier, let's not get ahead of the present. What we were trying to point out was the fact that you are not the first Predestine to feel insufficient, and Lord willing, you will not be the last."

"Elijah," Brutus continued, "your attitude is the reason you are the chosen one. You see, if you thought you were good enough to be the one, then you would definitely not be the one. However, you knowing that you cannot be the chosen one based on your own power opens up to you unlimited power in the service of the King. The King records this in His Word through one of the greatest defenders of all time: 'And he said unto me, My grace is sufficient for thee: for my strength is made perfect in weakness. Most gladly therefore will I rather glory in my infirmities, that the power of Christ may rest upon me. Therefore I take pleasure in infirmities, in reproaches, in necessities, in persecutions, in distresses for Christ's sake: for when I am weak, then am I strong.'"

"And in another place in the King's Word," added Zephyr. "'Not that we are sufficient of ourselves to think anything as of ourselves; but our sufficiency is of God.' So you see, it is not your own power that makes you the chosen one, but the power of the Great King."

Hearing the words of the King energized Eli's love and loyalty for the King and gave him confidence that perhaps he was wrong; maybe the King could make a defender out of him after all. Having settled the matter for the time, Eli consented to continue walking.

chapter 8
the courtyard of eden

For what it was worth, Eli enjoyed walking through the castle. Eli had always loved stories of the old days of knights and castles and always loved pretending to be a warrior fighting the forces of darkness. The castle, which looked like it had come directly from one of these fairy tales, fueled Eli's fire for adventure and his curiosity about this realm. The further the group walked down the hallway, the more warmth Eli could feel from the light of the realm. After another right turn, Eli understood where the extra warmth was coming from.

Not far from where the group turned right was a massive archway flanked by two white marble pillars that led into a courtyard outside the castle. The archway was taller and wider than the other doorways in the castle and was more elaborately decorated. Beautifully carved vines with gorgeous flowers wound up the pillars and connected to each other in the middle of the archway. The vines were carved out of what appeared to be pure emerald and the petals of the flowers were made up of other precious stones such as rubies, sapphires, and topazes. The sculpting of the vines and flowers was so perfect that the more Eli looked at the vines and flowers, the more it seemed to Eli that they were alive. Above the archway, in a font that gave the appearance of being woven by vines and inlayed with gold, were the words,

The Courtyard of Eden.

Ike continued leading the group out of the archway and into the light as he announced, "I present to you, the Courtyard of Eden."

The moment Eli stepped out into the light of the courtyard, an involuntary chuckle escaped his lips. The light felt amazing! Eli felt as if the light woke up his body from slumber, like a flower that had been in the shade finally getting the direct sunlight it craved. The light rejuvenated his body, cleared his mind, and made Eli feel as if his heart was on fire with love for the King.

"Wow, guys, this is amazing!" exclaimed Eli.

"Yes it is," replied Zephyr. "It is my favorite spot to come and enjoy the light of the King in this castle."

"Now," began Eli, "this isn't the *actual* Eden is it?"

"No, of course not," said Ike in a very tour-guide way. "This is merely an exact replica of the Eden the King created in the physical realm."

The Courtyard of Eden was a mix of pure white stone paths, luscious green grass, beautiful flowers, and fruit-bearing trees. The group descended three steps that led from the archway to a pure white stone path that cut through the incredibly green, luscious grass. Trying to take in as much as possible, Eli noticed that these trees not only produced much of the fruit Eli had eaten since his arrival, but they also produced fruit that he was accustomed to from the physical realm. The path led through the courtyard and to a large clearing in what Eli guessed to be the center of the courtyard. There, made entirely out of pure gold and sparkling in the light of the King, was the largest fountain Eli had ever seen. It was round, as large as a pond, and had a gigantic golden statue in the center. The statue looked like an eel mixed with a dragon. It had a long eel-like body with a large dorsal fin stretching the length of its back. The creature's head, which looked like a dragon's head, had two large horns above each eye and a mouth full of razor sharp teeth, each tooth the size of a large sword. It had a tail like an eel, but instead of flippers or fins, it had four legs with razor sharp talons the size of spears. The statue portrayed the creature jumping out of the water with golden fire spewing from its mouth. At the top of the golden fire, water shot into the sky creating a large umbrella of water that splashed down back into the fountain.

"Is that a dragon?" asked Eli, in awe of the sparkling statue.

"No, not a dragon," said Ike in an amused tone. "That, Master Storm, is the Leviathan. The Leviathan is an ancient creature that used to roam the seas of the physical realm. Though it is not what the physical realm calls a dragon, it was the inspiration to the stories from which your ideas of dragons come from."

After his initial awe of the fountain, Eli noticed that the fountain was like a golden sun lying in the center of the courtyard with several white paths leading from the fountain in all directions like sun-beams.

The sound of splashing caught Eli's attention and so he walked over to the edge of the golden fountain wondering what kind of fish he would find in this incredible place. To Eli's surprise, the water was crystal clear and empty of any fish or animals. Eli continued to watch the water to see if he was missing anything when a fish leapt out of the water and returned with a small splash. Eli's eyes widened. The fish was not a fish, but water in the shape of a fish. Eli stood motionless as the Angelos looked at each other barely containing their laughter. Finally, Zephyr spoke.

"Come, Eli, we have more important things to do than to observe the fountain."

"Yeah," said Eli, "but how—what I mean is—oh never mind."

The whole group laughed, even Ike who Eli was afraid might feel as if Eli were ruining his tour guide opportunity, and they continued their journey on the path that led to the northwest of the fountain toward an archway on the opposite side of the courtyard.

Still immensely enjoying the warmth of the King's light, Eli looked up and noticed for the first time that there was no visible source producing this light.

"Zeph?" asked Eli. "Where is the sun? I see the light, feel all the incredible benefits of the light, but I don't see where the light is coming from."

"In the spirit realm we do not have need of the sun; the King is our light and warmth. The light you see and the warmth you feel comes directly from the King's throne room."

"So what you're saying," answered Eli slowly, "is all the light in this realm, both inside and outside of the castle comes from the King's throne room? But how can that be?"

"Remember, Master Storm, you are in the spirit realm now. The spirit realm does not share the same boundaries and limits as does the physical realm. But as we have said, these are things you will get used to in time."

Eli was so engulfed with the light, the fountain, and the conversation with Zephyr that he did not realize until it was too late that the group was approaching a pride of lions that was crossing their path. Eli froze in place, afraid of getting eaten or attacked. As the lions crossed, a large male lion approached Eli. Not knowing if he should run or stand still, Eli stood there looking toward any of the Angelos for help.

"This is a perfect example of one of the differences I was speaking about," continued Zephyr as he flew next to Eli and petted the lion's head.

The lion produced a massive purring sound and looked to Eli wondering why he too was not joining in the petting. Slowly Eli lowered his hand and caressed the massive cat's head and mane. The lion gave them both a pleased look and licked Eli's hand with his large, sandpaper-like tongue before going back with his pride.

"These animals are not tainted with the curse of sin like the ones in the physical realm," said Zephyr. "They do not have the fear or aggression that the creatures in the physical realm have. One day, when the King makes everything new, what you just experienced will be experienced by all those to whom the King gives new life."

"Wow!" was all Eli could say as he was still relishing in the fact that he had just pet a lion.

"Here we are," announced Ike as he stopped before another large archway. "I present to you, the entrance to the Northwest Wing."

This archway was different from the one Eli entered in because instead of two white marble pillars, there were two black marble knights in full armor flanking the archway. The knights were also covered in carved emerald vines but instead of flowers, these vines produced swords, shields, and spears made from rubies, sapphires, and topazes. Above the archway, inlayed with gold, were the words,

The Northwest Wing.

Eli knew he was no expert on the spirit realm, but Eli did know by the looks of the archway, that whatever was in the Northwest Wing, he had better be ready for battle.

chapter 9
the choice of destiny

The group ascended the three marble stairs that led from the white path in Eden to the familiar white marble floor of the castle. Though the floor and wall color was familiar to Eli, it seemed to him that everything else about the Northwest Wing differed from the parts of the castle he had seen earlier.

Instead of the peaceful quiet atmosphere in the previous section of castle, this section was filled with movement and chatter. Armored Angelos flew in and out of doors and up and down the hallway at great speed. Every now and again, an Angelos would stop, bow, and greet the group before moving on. The hallway echoed with commands from what sounded like military commanders followed with the constant reply of, "Yes, Sir." Eli felt that this would be the atmosphere in the castle if the castle were under attack.

Not only was the atmosphere of the castle more war-like, but the decorations lining the walls also gave notice that this section of the castle was different. The decorations still included large portraits, suits of armor, and banners, only these suits of armor and banners had obviously seen actual combat. Many of the suits of armor had dents, dings, and scorch marks. Eli even saw one suit of armor in a case that had a soccer-ball-sized hole right through the midsection of the armor. Not sure how the person could have survived an attack like that, or even if the person did survive, Eli quickly walked past. The banners that hung from the ceiling also showed signs of battle. Many of the banners were torn and burnt. Some had been repaired, but many were still in their tattered condition.

The group approached a large, black, cast-iron, spiral staircase that ascended several stories to what appeared to be one of the towers of the castle. Flanking both sides of the staircase were armored Angelos hovering in place keeping guard. Eli realized that this was the first time he had seen any guards inside the castle and he concluded that where they were going must be extremely important. Ike nodded at the two guards who momentarily nodded back in response before returning their gaze forward allowing the group to ascend up the staircase.

After walking up four levels of stairs, passing a set of guards on each level, the group reached the top and stepped into a long hallway. Lining the walls of the hallway were beautiful crystal podiums that looked like the columns Eli saw on the ancient Greek temples. These podiums rose to about Eli's chest in height and had an item encased in a crystal cube. At the base of each podium was some type of laser light that shone into the crystal podium causing the podiums to change color from red, to blue, to green, to purple, to orange and covered the entire spectrum of the colors of the rainbow. Eli approached one of these podiums and spied what looked like some sort of animal horn attached to a leather strip. As he approached, golden letters etched into the crystal glowed with light and read, "The Trumpet of Gideon," and a hologram of a man standing on the peak of a hill blowing the trumpet in the dark of night with a torch in his other hand appeared on the backside of the crystal cube.

Stunned, Eli turned with his mouth open about to ask if this was really *the* trumpet of Gideon when he was cut off by Brutus' amused answer. "Yes, it is."

From that point on, Eli did not pass one artifact without stopping and reading the inscription and watching the hologram of the event from which that artifact came. Eli saw the stones and slingshot David used to kill Goliath, and after seeing the hologram of the giant, Eli realized that the estimates of Goliath's height were not exaggerated. They continued past the jawbone of a donkey with which Samson killed a thousand Philistines, the stray arrow that killed king Ahab, and the threatening letters sent from Sennacherib challenging king Hezekiah and the King to defy his power. The entire group paused before the podium with the letters from Sennacherib and watched the hologram of Hezekiah kneeling before the Lord and the Lord sending His angel to smite the Assyrians.

"You see there, Eli," said Brutus proudly. "That is what we call *Angelos dunamis*, or in English, the power of the messenger: what you all call angels."

Looking at these artifacts from the Bible, Eli realized that of all the portraits he had seen, he had not seen any of the characters from the Bible.

"Hey, Ike," enquired Eli. "Where are all the portraits of all the people we read about in the Bible?"

Ike turned and seemed exceptionally pleased to have an opportunity to answer a tour-guide-type question.

"The portraits that contain the heroes recorded in the King's Word are scattered throughout the different wings of the castle. Though the lives of these men and women are found in the Word, the King does not separate them from other defenders you do not find in the Word. The portraits of the Biblical heroes are side by side with the other defenders of their time. You see, the King honors all the men and women who rise up and become defenders equally. The King has no favorites; He perfectly loves all those who choose to honor Him."

"Incredible!" Eli replied. "Zeph said my grandfather's portrait is in the war room. Are we going to get a chance to see it?"

Smiling, Ike replied, "Why yes, Predestine Storm, we are going to the war room now. You have an appointment with the General and if we do not hurry, you will be late."

Ike proceeded to hurry the group down the remaining part of the hallway and toward two large black doors with golden hardware. Above the double-doors etched into the black marble walls gleaming with golden light was written,

THE WAR ROOM

There is no wisdom or understanding

or counsel against the LORD.

The horse is prepared for the day of battle,

but deliverance is of the LORD.

Proverbs 21:30-31

Flanking the double-doors were what Eli thought to be large black marble statues of warriors in full armor holding shields in their right hands and swords in their left hands. However, as the group approached, beams of light shot from the eyes of the warriors, scanning the approaching group. After the beams scanned the group as a whole, each warrior sheaved his sword and opened the large black door he stood next to.

Leading the group to the threshold of the war room, Ike proclaimed, "May I present to you, the war room. The war room, Predestine Storm, is the room in which all military operations from this castle are planned, organized, and executed. I now take my leave to fulfill other duties. God speed to you all, especially you, young Predestine Storm."

The group thanked Ike for his service and then proceeded into the war room, or—as Eli thought it looked like—the largest game of Battleship he had ever seen.

Walking into the war room was like walking into a giant cube. The walls were perfectly square and plain save for a giant green holographic screen that covered the entire left wall and a round watch tower built directly onto the far right wall. Winding up the watchtower, from the floor to the top, was a black marble staircase. The ceiling of the war room rose to a point like an upside-down waffle cone that told Eli they were in one of the top towers in the castle.

Facing the large green holographic screen, which kept switching from maps of the earth to maps of a land Eli did not recognize, were one hundred wooden desks lined up in ten perfect rows of ten desks. Sitting at the desks were Angelos whose armor differed from the other Angelos in that they wore colored capes. These sitting Angelos would watch different parts on the large screen as well as smaller holographic green screens that appeared on their desks, and then call out orders. These orders were the same orders that Eli could hear echoing throughout the Northwest Wing. When each order was issued, an Angelos standing next to the desk would salute, call out, "Yes Sir," and then fly away. Eli noticed that the Angelos flew out of the large tower window, vanishing with a burst of colored light, which coincided with the color of the individual Angelos' wings, hair, and eyes; or they flew through the wall of the castle on which the door was located as if the castle walls were made out of water.

"Zeph," whispered Eli, "what's going on here? What is all of this?"

"Well, as you know, this is where all our military action in this castle takes place. The large screen constantly scans both the physical realm and the spiritual realm surveying the movements of the Enemy and the movements of the King. When we pick up the different actions, the orders are sent to the individual desks of the captains, the seated Angelos, who hold the responsibility for that particular area. The captains then issue the orders from the general, whom you will meet shortly, to the Angelos who then carry out the orders. If the orders require action in the physical realm, the Angelos fly out the window, which is actually a portal to the physical realm. If the orders require action in the spirit realm the Angelos fly through the castle to the different portals that lead to the different lands in the spirit realm. In your case, since you appeared not far from our front gates, we flew through the castle and out the gates to retrieve you."

"So you all saw me appear?" asked Eli.

"Yes, in fact, when you appeared, the large screen exploded with light and the whole room actually sat in silence for a brief moment before we saw the presence of the Enemy appear not far behind you," cut in Brutus who was listening to their conversation. "Your arrival followed by the Enemy's arrival was so shocking that I thought Captain Flintrock," whispered Brutus, pointing to one of the desks toward the back of the room behind which sat an Angelos with bushy eyebrows and a bushy mustache wearing a bright yellow cape, "was going to pick up his sword and come after you personally."

"So I'm guessing that you two were just the next Angelos in line when the orders came in to help me?" asked Eli to Zephyr.

"No, not exactly," Zephyr responded. "Brutus was next in line but when they realized who you were, they sent for me to meet up with them. You see, I am not a warrior Angelos. I am a guardian Angelos."

"I knew it!" exclaimed Eli. "You are my guardian Angelos! That is why you seem so familiar isn't it? Isn't it?"

"Yes, Eli," replied Zephyr. "I am your guardian Angelos. And yes," continued Zephyr before Eli could ask the same questions as before, "this has something to do with what might or might not happen depending on the choices you make. But no, we are not going to discuss it right now."

Feeling like a detective who just discovered a clue, Eli wanted to pursue the topic more, but stopped when he realized the war room had gone suddenly quiet. Eli looked up and noticed that all of the Angelos were staring at him with a look of wonder and curiosity. Just then an Angelos with light pink coloring approached the group.

"Ah yes, Zephyr, Brutus, and the young Predestine Storm. It is an honor to have you with us safely. It is not often that we have to snatch a Predestine from the literal jaws of the Enemy. I will inform Michael of your presence. Please wait here."

"Thanks Smitty," replied Brutus.

The Angelos named Smitty then flew up the staircase of the watchtower on the right wall and disappeared from

Eli's sight. Facing a room full of Angelos looking at him in admiration made Eli incredibly uncomfortable.

"Eli," whispered Zephyr, "they are staring at you because—"

"I know," interrupted Eli. "Because I am the chosen one. I get it Zeph."

"Yes and no," replied Zephyr. "You are the chosen one, but you look a lot like the last defender who entered these doors: your grandfather."

Zephyr pointed to a portrait that hung just above the entrance to the room. In all the excitement of the war room, Eli had forgotten that Ike told him that his grandfather's portrait was located in here. Looking at it in amazement, Eli saw his grandfather—not the older man whom Eli was familiar with, but a much younger version of him decked out in a gorgeous suit of armor, that to Eli's delight, matched the colors of Eli's suit. The portrait was as large as the other portraits and was also in an elaborate golden frame that looked amazing against the black marble wall. At the bottom of the portrait was an inscription plate that read:

Master Defender David Granite.

Defender of the poor, helper to the widows,

a light in the darkness.

A faithful servant of the Great King.

the calling

Even though Eli did not fully understand everything his grandfather did, he knew that his grandfather did something great and Eli was proud to be his grandson.

"Why does he look so young?" asked Eli.

"It is the spirit realm," replied Zephyr. "Your soul is not bound by the aging of your body. Though your grandfather's physical body was old, his soul is vibrant with the life of the King."

"Please don't take this the wrong way," Eli began cautiously, not wanting this question to sound negative toward his grandfather. "With all of the great accomplishments the men and women in the portraits accomplished, why is my grandfather's portrait in the War Room?"

"The location of Master Granite's portrait does not necessarily have to do with his accomplishments," cut in Brutus. "Your grandfather was the last defender who protected this region. When a defender moves on in the service of the King, the defender's portrait is placed here as a reminder that we Angelos are not in this fight alone and it also encourages us as we hope and pray the King sends us the next defender. Now that you are here, we will move your grandfather's portrait to another location. Well, I guess I should state that depending on your decision, we will move your grandfather's portrait."

At that moment, Smitty, the Angelos with the pink coloring returned. "General Michael desires to speak with you now, Predestine Storm. Please follow me."

Smitty led Eli through the center row of the desks. As he passed, Eli was greeted and cheered by the Angelos and their captains alike. As Eli walked passed Flintrock's desk, he could hear Flintrock talking about how he was reaching for his sword and about to take the Enemy head on when he saw Eli being chased. Eli did not know why, but seeing such familiar human traits in the Angelos made him smile.

Smitty led Eli all the way to the base of the winding staircase on the watchtower built into the right wall. As Eli walked up the stairs, he turned to ask Zephyr another question when he realized Zephyr and Brutus remained at the bottom of the stairs.

"Aren't you guys coming?" asked Eli a little more desperately than he wanted to sound.

"I am afraid not," said Zephyr. "The general desires to speak with you alone. But don't fear, Eli. If he doesn't like you, your death will be quick and painless."

Zephyr held back his smile for as long as he could before he and Brutus both burst out in laughter.

Eli shook his head at them. "Funny guys, real funny."

Not able to contain his smile any longer, Eli turned and followed Smitty up the staircase and to a large wooden door. The door was not nearly as extravagant as Eli would picture the door to the general's office. It was large, over ten feet high and five feet wide, but it was made out of a plain brown wood with black iron hardware.

Smitty hovered in front of the door and knocked once. The door swung in, squeaking as it did so. Smitty bowed to Eli. "Enter Predestine and choose your destiny."

"Thanks," replied Eli, a little stunned by the gravity of Smitty's statement.

Taking a deep breath, Eli walked into the general's office.

To Eli's amazement, the general's office was not as massive or as lavishly decorated as the other rooms in the castle. The room was a half-circle with the door he walked in on the round side of the wall facing the flat wall. There was no ceiling, but the room opened up on top to the ceiling of the war room.

In front of the flat wall facing the door was a very large, plain, white-stone desk with a massive white-stone chair sitting behind it. On top of the desk were several miniature hologram maps of all the maps on the large screen out in the war room and a statue that Eli had seen before. The statue was of Michael's battle with Satan.

In the right corner of the room, Eli's left as he walked in, against the flat wall was a giant golden spear hovering in mid-air. The spear must have been at least nine feet long with a gigantic spear head. The shaft of the spear was as thick as the business end of Eli's baseball bat.

I would not want to be the enemy of the guy who carries that spear, thought Eli.

Just then the door closed behind him revealing a gigantic muscular man in glowing white robes and a golden breastplate.

"Welcome, Predestine!" boomed the large angel. "I am Michael, servant of the Great King."

Michael extended his hand for Eli to shake but Eli was so shocked by the sudden appearance and power of Michael that he just looked at him.

"Is it not the custom of the physical realm to shake hands when greeting friends?" asked Michael.

"Um, yes," said Eli sheepishly as he extended his hand and shook Michael's massive hand. "I'm sorry, I just wasn't expecting you to be so big and be standing behind the door."

"I apologize for startling you," said Michael as he walked toward the desk. "Please come and sit down."

When Michael invited Eli to sit down, he waived his hand and a much smaller white-stone chair appeared facing the stone desk. Eli accepted Michael's invitation to sit down and while the angel walked around to the other side of the desk, Eli took a moment to examine Michael.

Michael was huge, at least eight-to-nine-feet tall and had to weigh around five hundred pounds if angels had weight. Not only was Michael huge, he was also the epitome of manly. Michael had bulging muscles, strong cheek bones, radiant blue eyes, and golden curly hair. Eli thought that Michael resembled the way mythology described Hercules.

Michael sat down behind his desk and with a wave of his right hand, the holographic maps disappeared. The large angel smiled at Eli in a way that calmed Eli's fear and shock at Michael's presence. Eli had no idea how Michael was able to do it, but there was something about the angel that made Eli feel safe and even comfortable in his presence even though the angel could squash him like a bug.

"I must say," began Michael, looking at Eli with excitement, "it is wonderful to finally have you here with us. It is a very rare happening when two successive defenders come from the same family. I admit that ever since Gabriel brought word to me from the King about His plan to choose you as your grandfather's successor, that I have been eager to meet you and to see in what ways you and your grandfather are alike and in what ways you are different. Now that you are sitting in front of me, I understand why the King would do something as rare as He has and to make you the next Predestine.

"It is with great joy that I inform you, Elijah Douglas Storm, that the Great King of all creation has personally chosen you to take up the title of Master Defender and to defend the realms of creation from the workings and the servants of the Enemy. You are the chosen one who is given this chance to follow in the footsteps of Master Defender Granite and become a great hero of the faith.

"Since the promotion of your grandfather, the Great King has allowed the Enemy's wicked servants to wage war in both the spiritual and physical realms. As a result, many of the peoples who inhabit this land are battling the cruel nature of the Enemy. You have been chosen by the King to battle the Enemy and his minions in the realms for the King. Now, before we go any further, do you have any questions for me?"

Eli leaned forward in his surprisingly comfortable stone chair. "I just don't understand why the King wants me. I mean, I know I am not a scholar or anything when it comes to the King's Word, but I do know enough to know that He is all-powerful and that He has the ability to blast the Enemy and all of his servants away. I just don't understand why the King would want me to be part of His army when He has warriors like you. Why does He not just step in and blast the Enemy away, or why don't you go and help the peoples of this realm? I am sure that you could do a way better job than me."

Michael smiled. "The King can destroy the Enemy and his servants with a word from His mouth. The King has declared that one day He will judge and punish the Enemy for all of his treachery and wickedness; however, until the King's perfect time of performing this act, He desires to ordain humans as defenders to defend this realm. As for me, I am currently participating in warfare against the Enemy and his servants, just not in the same capacity that you are called to serve. One day, when the King gives the command, I will be more active in the destruction of the Enemy. In fact, the King's word declares that I will have the opportunity to go one-on-one with the Enemy."

Michael's countenance flashed with a bright light as Michael cracked his knuckles and tilted his head toward the statue on his desk.

"Hold up," said Eli, a little amused. "You keep a statue of yourself fighting the Enemy on your desk?"

"Yes I do," said Michael with a smile on his face. "Do you have a problem with that?" Michael asked as he sat back in his chair placing his hands behind his head flexing his gargantuan biceps.

"Um, nope," replied Eli. "No problem at all."

They both laughed before Michael continued. "Until the King gives those orders, my orders are to help train and assist the defenders of the King in their mission. You see, the King delights to use humans because for a human to accept the call requires great faith. As you will come to learn, Eli, there is no greater source of joy and honor for the King than the faith His people place in Him.

"I know it is impossible for you to completely understand at this time," Michael continued. "But you will understand more and more as you continue in your journey if you so choose to accept it. What you need to know right now is that the King who is perfect in all His ways specifically chose and gifted you for this mission. This is your mission to accept or reject. This is the King's plan for your life; however, you do not have to accept it. You can choose to turn down this mission and we will return you to the physical realm the exact moment in time you entered the spirit realm. You would not be the first Predestine who chose to reject the mission of the King and you would certainly not be the last. In His Sovereign Majesty, the King allows you to make the choice. Master Elijah Storm, will you choose to accept this mission and serve the Great King?"

Michael leaned forward on his desk in anticipation and Eli could hear the large stone desk creak a little under the massive weight of Michael's upper body.

This is it, thought Eli as he leaned back in his chair.

Eli's mind raced through everything that had happened since the morning he woke up in his grandfather's house. Eli felt his newfound love and loyalty for the King surge through his body. Eli knew that the King had been patient with him all those years while Eli rejected Him. Eli knew that the King had not only saved him but had saved his grandfather before him. Yes, Eli was a little afraid of what accepting this invitation might mean—whether it was the enemies he would have to face or the pressure that would be placed upon him to live up to his grandfather's reputation, but the love for the King overshadowed everything.

The King not only created Eli, but He also gave Eli new life through the shedding of His own blood. Now, the King has chosen Eli to become a defender and have an opportunity to honor the King with his life. Eli did not have to think long before he looked back at an expectant Michael.

"I don't understand everything but I do understand that with everything the King has done for me, I would be a fool to turn down the honor of following my grandfather and becoming a defender for the King. I would be honored to accept my mission for the King and follow my grandfather as the defender of this realm."

Michael's being once again flashed with light and he clapped his hands sending a booming noise throughout the room. "Praise the King! I knew the love of the King was strong in you. There is no time to lose! Your training begins now!"

chapter 10
the guardian's questions

Michael stood up so fast that his chair crashed into the wall behind him, creating several giant cracks in the wall. Immediately the wall mended itself and the chair returned to its place behind Michael.

"Don't worry about that," said a jubilant Michael. "It happens more than you might think. Come now, get up, we have much to accomplish."

"What do you mean?" asked Eli, a little surprised by Michael's quick response to his acceptation. "What are we going to do now?"

"First," Michael began as he walked around his desk, "we must inform the anxious Angelos in the war room that you have accepted the task. Second, we need to begin your mission training right away. If you desire to become a Master Defender, then you must prove yourself worthy."

"Whoa!" exclaimed Eli. "I thought accepting the mission made me a Master Defender. No one said anything about having to prove myself worthy."

"No, Predestine Storm, accepting the mission places you in training. To become a Master Defender and take up the role of defender of this realm, you must first complete a mission that will test you in a way that will reveal if you are truly ready to become a Master Defender. But do not worry, I have complete confidence in you and I will explain more as we make our way to the atrium. For now, arise and let us share the victory of your decision with the war room."

Eli rose from his chair and followed Michael to the large door which Michael opened. The two exited the door and stood at the top of the black marble stairway. Their appearance brought the war room to an instant state of calm and quiet. Placing his massive arm around Eli, Michael announced, "I am thrilled to communicate to you all that Predestine Storm has accepted the King's call to become the next Master Defender of this realm!"

The calm and quiet of the war room erupted into cheers and loud applause. Eli followed Michael down the staircase where Zephyr and Brutus were the first to congratulate him.

"I knew you would make the right decision," said Zephyr.

"Yes," butted in Brutus. "Your grandfather told us you were too much of a sucker for an adventure to turn down an opportunity like this. I'm glad to see that he was right."

"I don't understand," said Eli. "Why is everyone so excited? Did you all really think that I, or anyone for that matter, who is given this opportunity would actually turn it down?"

"That is exactly what we thought," said Michael. "For that is exactly what has happened many times in the past and will happen many more times until the King brings His judgment upon the Enemy."

"You mean that others have actually said no to the King?"

"Yes," said Michael with sorrow in his voice. "There are many believers living their lives in the physical realm who were called to become defenders and live a life that influences both realms for the King who turned it down for one reason or another. This is why you must complete this first mission. Your first mission will test your resolve and commitment to the King. It is this first mission that many prospective defenders have failed to accomplish."

"I don't want to sound prideful or anything," replied Eli. "But personally I think a person would have to be crazy to turn down the opportunity to serve the King and make Him proud."

"I agree!" replied Michael. "But as you can see from our reaction to your acceptance, it is a common thing. The Angelos are cheering not just because you chose to accept, but because it is a rare thing to have two defenders accept the mission back to back. The King is doing something great with you, Predestine. Not only are you following a defender of your own kin, but you are following immediately. This is indeed a rare thing. I am looking forward to seeing what the King has in store for you. Your grandfather will be very proud when he finds out."

Eli felt an uncontrollable smile stretch across his face at the thought of someone telling his grandfather about Eli's choice to follow in his steps. While the Angelos were coming up and congratulating Eli on his acceptance, Michael turned toward the staircase, and with a swish of his hand, the staircase rotated giving the tower the appearance of an old barber-shop sign.

"Come, Eli, the atrium is this way," said Michael as he walked toward the base of the tower.

Eli followed and as he walked up beside Michael the bottom section of the tower's base rotated revealing a long white-marble stairwell that stretched downward into the castle. As the King's light flooded the staircase, torches mounted on the walls lit with a golden fire further illuminated the way ahead of them. The opening and the staircase looked as if they were built to accommodate Michael. The door and stairwell looked to be a perfect ten-by-ten foot square that would allow Michael enough room to walk down the stairs comfortably with a person at his side.

The revealing of the stairwell seemed to pass the message along to the Angelos who were congratulating Eli as they returned in unison to their duties in the war room.

"Zephyr," said Michael, "I am taking Elijah to the Atrium. When I return we will begin to prepare you for the future."

Eli's eyes shot open in surprise.

"Yes, Elijah," said Zephyr with a large smile on his face as he watched Eli's eyes widen at Michael's comments. "This has everything to do with your choice to accept the King's calling."

Before Eli could speak, Michael's booming voice grabbed his attention. "Come with me," said Michael as he took the lead down the staircase.

Eli walked beside Michael down the spiraling marble staircase. After a few moments of silence, Eli asked, "So this first mission, you said it would test my resolve to see if I am really ready to be a defender. What did you mean by that?"

Without turning to look at Eli, Michael replied, "Well, Predestine, to become a defender takes more than just a desire to become a defender and more than just a verbal acceptance of the King's call. It requires a level of faith that motivates you to follow the King's orders no matter what the personal cost. I am not permitted to tell you any more than this: the only person keeping you from being a defender is you."

"Me?" questioned Eli as if he did not hear Michael properly. "What do you mean I am the only person keeping me from becoming a defender?"

"I am sorry, Eli, I cannot tell you more. You will learn this truth and what it means to you as you progress through your first mission. And the time of your first mission is rapidly approaching."

Michael finished his sentence as the stairwell spilled into a short hallway with a door at the end of it. Standing next to the door was a full-body suit of armor complete with a round shield in its left steel gauntlet and a sword hilt in its right. Eli thought it was curious that the sword had no blade but before he could think upon it too deeply, his attention leapt to the door. The door was exactly one foot shorter than the hallway, standing about nine feet and was only about five feet wide, but it was made out of a smooth sheet of solid gold. Eli did not see any door handle or door hardware but he did not care, because the solid gold sheet reflected the light of the King making the door look as if it were glowing like the sun.

Michael and Eli approached the door and stopped just a few steps away from the armor. Before Eli could ask Michael what they were waiting for or how they would get through the door, the golden light that lit the torches on the wall of the stairwell flew out of their torches and poured into the armor. The armor gave a jolt and then came to life.

The armor stepped forward out of its position and rolled its neck the same way Eli did in the morning when he fell asleep in an awkward position. The armor then took its sword hand and lifted its facial visor up revealing a face of golden fire. The face looked humanoid with a mouth, nose, and eyes. The armor's eyes met Eli's and Eli felt as if the armor could see right through him. Not being able to look away from the armor's eyes, Eli jumped when he heard Michael's booming voice.

"Guardian, we have come to seek permission to enter the sacred Atrium of Ephesdammim."

The golden fire eyes of the Guardian looked to Michael and its face smiled brightly.

"Welcome, Michael, mighty warrior of the King!" boomed the guardian.

"Thank you, old friend," replied Michael. "It has been many years."

"Nearly a thousand years if I am not mistaken," replied the guardian.

"You are not mistaken, my friend, but I have a surprise for you."

Michael placed his hand on Eli's shoulder and the guardian once again looked at Eli. Eli froze as he felt the fiery eyes examine him. The suit of armor cracked a smile and looked back at Michael.

"You don't say! Standing before me is the grandson of Master Defender Granite!"

Eli smiled at the mentioning of his grandfather. "You knew my grandfather?"

The guardian continued smiling. "Correction, I know your grandfather, and yes, he was the last defender whom I allowed entrance. Your grandfather has since done very well for the King and I see the same spirit and potential in you!"

Michael smiled. "May I present to you Elijah Storm. Elijah this is the guardian of the Atrium of Ephesdammim."

"Nice to meet you, sir," said Eli in the best confident voice he could muster. "But what is the Atrium of Ephes-da-mmin ?"

"Ah, young defender," spoke the guardian. "The Atrium of Ephesdammim is a room full of wonder and mystery. It is the main war room for defenders of the King in their battle against the cursed Enemy. In this room are portals that will take you to different lands all throughout the spirit realm. Defenders travel through these portals and face the servants of the Enemy in battle for the glory of the King."

"Okay," said Eli as he nodded his head. "But what does Ephes-da-mmin mean? Or do I really want to know?"

The guardian chuckled. "Ephesdammim is the name of the battlefield on which the great Defender David triumphed over the infidel Goliath. The spirit and courage Master Defender David displayed in his trust of the power of the King to confront a devastating enemy we thought to be a fitting analogy for this room. You see, those who are permitted to enter the atrium must face powerful enemies. These enemies have power far greater than the defender; however, these enemies have no power against the King. Only those defenders who are courageous enough to confront these enemies while trusting the King for the victory will enter and be successful. To enter this room, you must be willing to enter your own Ephesdammim and face what the physical realm calls, 'impossible odds.'"

Michael added, "It is one thing to accept the calling of the King, and another thing to enter the Atrium of Ephesdammim. The men and women who step through this door proclaim that they are ready to step onto the field of battle. So Elijah, are you ready to take your grandfather's place as the King's defender for this realm?"

"Yes!" replied Eli immediately.

The guardian nodded. "Acceptance without any hesitation. You are a lot like your grandfather. Now before I allow you entrance, you must answer two questions. First, why do you seek entrance into the Atrium of Ephesdammim?"

The question caught Eli off guard. It was a simple question, and yet, Eli searched his mind for several moments and could not come up with what he felt would be a sufficient answer. After several strained moments, Eli looked the guardian in the fiery eyes and spoke.

"I don't really know. In all honesty, I did not realize what the atrium was five minutes ago. I have not had time to fully digest all the things you have told me about the atrium, nor have I had time to prepare myself for what is inside the atrium. All I know is that I want nothing more than to serve the Great King. Ever since the King redeemed me, I want nothing more than to please Him. I desire to go to the atrium because I know that is where He desires I go. If the atrium were a basement, dungeon, or any other place, I would gladly follow the King's lead for my life. I want to go where the King wants me to go and right now that is the Atrium of Ephesdammim."

With a smile of satisfaction the guardian spoke. "Well said, young Master. With a heart like that, you will bring great glory to the King. I look forward to hearing about the great victories the King will grant you.

"Now for the second question. Are you ready to face the impossible for the King?"

This second question did not sit well with Eli. Eli was not sure why, but something about the question offended him. As Eli thought about the question and why it was troubling him, he saw what he thought was a glimmer escape from the Bible in its sheaf on his belt. Curious, Eli reached over and touched the Bible. Immediately a verse sprung into his mind.

But Jesus looked at them and said,

"With men it is impossible,

but not with God; for with God

all things are possible."

Mark 10:27

Eli shuddered as a warm sensation swept through his body.

"Nothing is impossible with God. The Bible says that the things which are impossible with men are possible with God. You asked if I was ready to face the impossible for the King but your question does not make sense because with the King nothing is impossible. I don't understand your question."

The guardian looked taken back. "Well I'll be a can-opener's cousin! Michael, did you just see what I saw?"

"I certainly did!" boomed Michael as he looked at Eli in wonder. "I do believe we just witnessed the true potential Eli has for the King."

"Potential?" interrupted Eli. "What do you mean? What did you see?"

"We saw you connect with the King's Word," said the guardian. "Something that does not happen with most defenders until they are well into their training. In fact, if my memory serves me, there has been only one other defender who stood before that had a similar connection with the King's Word to answer my questions. That defender was a shepherd boy named David. Have you heard of him? You have just demonstrated that your potential for the King is no less than his."

The guardian shook himself back in an official position.

"Predestine Storm, you have answered my questions in an acceptable manner and so by the power invested in me by the Almighty King, I allow you entrance into the Atrium of Ephesdammim."

The guardian lifted his sword hilt hand and golden flame burst from the hilt forming the blade of the sword. He then turned and thrust the golden flame sword into the golden door. In moments the door was a golden liquid with the consistency of Jell-O.

Still in his professional manner, the guardian addressed Eli once more.

"Enter now, Elijah Storm, and battle bravely for the King."

"You mean you want me to walk through the liquid door?" asked Eli.

"Unless you know a different way," said the guardian, trying to maintain his professional manner but giving Eli a wink.

Michael placed his hand on Eli's back and gently directed him toward the door.

"It is always a pleasure to see you again, old friend," said Michael to the guardian. "Perhaps we can join together again in battle one day soon if the King wills."

"I look forward to that day!" replied the guardian. "And as always, the pleasure is mine, my friend."

Eli walked to the rippling gold door and tested it by placing his hand against it. His hand went right through as if he were placing his hand through a swimming pool. Eli quickly retrieved his hand before looking to Michael for the okay. Michael nodded, and Eli walked through the door and entered the Atrium of Ephesdammim.

chapter 11
the atrium

There could not have been a greater contrast in Eli's mind than to walk through a liquid golden door glowing with the light of the King only to step into the Atrium of Ephesdammim. The door was bright, warm, and glowing with the light of the King, whereas the atrium was dark, cold, and absent of all life.

Eli felt as if he had just walked into an old black-and-white television show that had been frozen in time. Everything in this room except for Eli and Michael was void of any color, life, or movement. All the elements of this once majestic room looked as if time had frozen them in place.

The atrium was a large rectangular room about the size of a football field. The walls of the Atrium were made out of what Eli thought was stained glass, but because they were mainly covered in vines, and because there was no color in the room, he could not be certain. The roof of the atrium was made out of frosted crystal through which the light of the King still illuminated this room, allowing Eli to see that even the dust particles visible in the light beams of the King were frozen in place.

Eli took a moment to look around at this mysterious room. Flanking both sides of the door he walked through were small waterfalls that poured out of the mouths of stone lions protruding out from the walls about midway up the walls. The water was frozen and mist-spray from the once falling water was also frozen giving the waterfalls a very 3-D effect. The water from the waterfalls poured into two small streams that ran parallel to each other the length of the room and then, to Eli's amazement, looked as if they ascended up the far wall and back into the mouths of two other stone lions.

Seven white gazebos were spread throughout the atrium. Six of these gazebos were small, and broken up symmetrically with three on the left side of the two streams and three on the right side of the two streams. The small gazebos were made of a white stone that appeared to have glitter mixed into the stone that sparkled in the light of the King. The small gazebos were round with a dome roof and had six pillars. Inside the small gazebos was just enough room for one to two people to stand. Connecting each little gazebo with the main strip of land between the two streams were crystal bridges that arched in the middle allowing the stream to flow freely underneath.

Sitting in the center of the room, in between the two streams, was the large gazebo. The large gazebo was also made of the same white sparkly stone with a dome roof and pillars, only this gazebo had twenty-four pillars. Inside this gazebo was more than enough room for several people to move freely.

The eerie stillness of the room added to Eli's shock when Michael's booming voice broke the silence.

"Welcome, Predestine Storm, to the Atrium of Ephesdammim. This room will serve as your command center as you fulfill your mission from the King. From this room, you will travel to the lands of the spiritual realm, as well as the physical realm, and will meet the Enemy and his minions in battle."

"And what is my mission exactly?" inquired Eli.

"Your mission, Eli, is to equip yourself with the spiritual armor the Great King has provided for all His defenders. This armor was specially forged by the Great King and is empowered by His might. By attaining this armor, you will gain the power and the knowledge you need to become a great defender of the realms."

"So where is this armor and how do I get it?"

"The pieces of armor are being held by different servants of the Enemy. In order for you to retrieve the pieces of armor, you must travel to the different lands and defeat the Enemy's servants. This room will be your guide. Each small gazebo is a portal to a specific land in which a part of the armor is being held. When you are ready, the portal that you must go through will light up and take you to where you need to go. It is only as you complete each mission and equip each piece of armor that you will gain the strength to fulfill the next task and become a great defender for the King."

"What about that large gazebo in the middle?" asked Eli.

"That is the portal that will lead you back to the physical realm when your mission calls for it. Remember, a defender defends both the physical and spirit realms. Your missions will not only include spirit realm battles, but the battles in the physical realm."

For the first time, Eli felt the weight of the mission before him. Taking a moment to think about everything Michael said, Eli looked around the room once more.

After a moment to think about everything, Eli spoke. "I just want to make sure I understand what you are saying. The King has made a suit of armor for me that I need to defeat the Enemy and his servants. However, the pieces of my armor are currently being held captive by different enemies spread all throughout the spirit realm. My mission is to go and somehow defeat these creatures, help the people under attack, and gain the armor."

"Yes, Eli, that is correct."

"Then, as I progress through this mission to acquire the armor, I will still have battles and responsibilities to fight the Enemy and his workings in the physical realm as well."

"Yes again, Eli, you are correct."

"Michael, I just don't know if I have what you need to be the next great defender of the realms. I guess I am just a little nervous that I am going to go into one of these portals with a lot of people counting on me only to fail them and fail you, or go back to the physical realm and continue to fail the King as I have failed Him for years. Are you sure that I am the one who is meant to be the next defender of the realms?"

Michael knelt down so that he was about eye level with Eli.

"I understand your concern, Eli. What you need to know is that there are no accidents, ever. The Great King chose you and called you to be the next defender and we know that He does not make mistakes. You have everything you need to be a great defender because you have the calling of the King. Further, you have a promise from the King that He has put in His Word to give you comfort in times like these. Eli, you are already more than prepared to be successful because you already have a connection with the King's Word. I want you to focus again, like you did when you answered the guardian's question, and I want you to tell me what promise the King has given you in His Word."

Eli took the Bible his grandfather left him and thumbed through the pages. Closing his eyes, Eli thought about promises that might be in the Bible. Eli felt a little tingling in his chest and a small pin-hole of light appeared in the darkness behind his closed eyelids. That pin-hole grew rapidly as if Eli's mind were being sucked into the hole until his mind was engulfed with a bright light. Then the words filled his mind with such power it forced Eli to open his eyes and look down. The Bible had opened itself and there in front of him was the passage of Scripture that burned into his mind. The verses were glowing with the same light that filled his mind, highlighting the words on the page.

This Book of the Law shall not

depart from your mouth,

but you shall meditate in it day and night,

that you may observe to do

according to all that is written in it.

For then you will make your way prosperous,

and then you will have good success.

Have I not commanded you?

Be strong and of good courage;

do not be afraid, nor be dismayed,

for the LORD your God is with you

wherever you go.

Joshua 1:8-9

A warm confidence spilled over Eli as if it were a bucket of water being poured on his head.

"Amazing!" exclaimed Eli as he was trying to convey his feelings over what had just happened. "I was just thinking about promises and then this passage engulfs my mind like fire and then I look down and my Bible is open to this very passage. How did that happen?"

"That, Eli," said a smiling Michael, "is the connection you have with the King's Word. We will have time to explain it more after your first mission, but your ability to already connect with the Word is unique among defenders. It is as the guardian said: we have not seen a defender have the same powerful connection with the King's Word before the training has begun since the time of David. Understand that the King's Word is the greatest weapon in all creation, and it is what gives you the ability to overcome the Enemy. If you know nothing else than you have a unique ability to wield the Word, then you need to know that you have more than most defenders have ever dreamed of having at this point in their training, including your grandfather."

Michael smiled, stood back up, and looked toward the gazebos.

"We have come to the time of your mission. Eli, do you have enough faith to believe that you are chosen by the King to fulfill His mission for you?"

"Yes," said Eli.

"And do you believe that your King has given you all you need to be successful through the power of the King's Word?"

"Yes."

"Then, Master Storm, it is time for you to take your faith in the King and in His Word and step out into the battle field. Are you ready to accept your first mission and claim not only a piece of the King's armor but the title of defender of the realms?"

"Yes I am, Michael."

"Then step forward and face your mission in grace, faith, and power!"

Michael motioned for Eli to walk beside him as he walked between the two frozen streams toward the gazebos.

"Michael," asked Eli as they walked, "what happened to this room? Why is everything frozen in time and why does it not have any color?"

"I am glad that you asked that question. The condition of this room mirrors that of the condition of the lands in the spirit realm. Currently, without a defender serving the King in this region of the spiritual realm, this region is as if it were frozen in time. The continual growth that occurs through the honoring of the King has been hindered by the presence of the Enemy and his servants. The great joy that accompanies the closeness to the King represented by the beautiful colors and sweet odors that fill this room has been slowly sapped through the evil workings of the Enemy. This room is a picture of the state of this region in the spiritual and physical realms. This room needs a hero to come and restore its grandeur, life, and beauty just as the realms need a hero to restore their grandeur, life, and beauty. Eli, the King has called you to be that hero. As you progress through your missions, you will see the great difference you are making as you watch this room transform into what it was created to be."

Michael finished speaking as the two of them arrived at the first part of the semicircle of gazebos. Suddenly, a ray of light appeared underneath their feet and spread to their left as if the room were drawing a line with yellow light toward the crystal bridge that connected the mainland with the first gazebo on the left. When the light hit the bridge, the bridge's crystal erupted with the light filling the darkened space around the bridge with brilliant color. The line of light proceeded until it reached the gazebo which also erupted with the light. Knowing that the room had directed Eli where to go, Eli turned toward Michael with one last question.

"Michael, how will I know what to do, or where to go when I get where I am going?"

"Don't worry about that," said Michael. "The King has allowed your grandfather to leave you directions on your first mission, then after you succeed, you will have company who will go with you on your future missions. But we will talk about that more after you return victoriously. Eli, I am proud to have been able to meet you and assist you. I have confidence that the King will lead you to victory. Now go, and I will be waiting for you when you return."

Michael moved his massive arm in the direction of the light path and Eli knew that the time had come for him to begin his mission for the King. Taking a deep breath, Eli walked on the path, over the bridge, and into the gazebo. When Eli reached the center of the gazebo, his grandfather's ring on his finger lit up with an emblem of a helmet. Immediately, that same helmet emblem appeared above his head in the same yellow light that led from the mainland to the gazebo. The light from the path flooded the gazebo floor, swirling as it rose up to the domed roof sealing Eli into the gazebo. When the light filled the dome, a beam of light shot from the top of each of the six pillars and met in the center of the dome forming a growing ball of light around the helmet. Eli raised his right arm to shield his eyes as he looked upward when the ball of light shot a large beam of light at Eli. The light beam hit Eli in his lifted arm turning his arm into light. The light spread until Eli's body was nothing more than the bright yellow light. Eli felt his whole body radiate with energy and then Eli was sucked into the yellow ball of light. Instantly, the gazebo went back to its former state and Eli was nowhere to be found.

chapter 12
the cemetery of the old man

Travelling through portals was definitely one of Eli's new favorite activities. Eli felt as if he were a speck of dust being sucked up by a vacuum cleaner. He could feel himself soaring through space being pulled to the right and then to the left. Eli thought the whole sensation must be what an electrical current goes through when a person flips a light switch and the current is sent through the wiring to the light bulb. After a few brief moments of soaring through space, Eli felt solid ground under his feet and watched as his body reformed from the light starting at his feet and continuing up to his head.

The light that had engulfed his body returned to the ball of light hovering in the dome roof of the gazebo and then shot into the ground outside the gazebo forming another path of light that stretched from the gazebo about twenty feet and then cut to the left up a large hill.

Eli noticed that, though the gazebo was identical to the one he stepped into in the atrium, he was not in the atrium any longer. Two aspects about his location communicated this fact right away. First Eli noticed the darkness. The gazebo had light inside of it enough for Eli to see, but surrounding the gazebo and filling this new land was a thick, ink-like darkness.

The darkness was eerie, but the bone-chilling wind was what unsettled Eli's nerves. Though the gazebo kept the darkness at bay, it did nothing to protect Eli from the ice-cold wind. Eli had not taken one step into this new land and already he felt that this world was made up of the same elements one would find at a haunted hayride. Only, Eli knew that nothing on a hayride could hurt him. Here, however, Eli had no such guarantee. Eli knew that the Enemy and his servants were very real, very capable of hurting him, and that he was now on their turf.

Feeling a sense of security in the gazebo, Eli walked around inside the gazebo to see this new land in which his mission lay. One thought came to mind as he surveyed what he could see through the darkness: death.

The ground was covered in grass, only it was all dead grass. There were no flowers or even weeds mixed into the grass; there was only dead grass. Flanking both sides of the path of light were several trees that looked as though they were designed by a horror-movie director. The bark of the trees was black, like the tree-had-been-burned-with-fire black. There were no leaves on the trees and all the dead branches looked like they were razor-sharp claws just waiting for the chance to grab an unsuspecting passer-by.

Well, I can't stay in the gazebo forever, Eli thought to himself as he gathered up his courage and stepped out of the gazebo onto the path of light.

Cautiously, Eli walked down the path and turned left to walk up the hill.

"What in the world are you doing here?" called a voice from the tree on Eli's right.

Eli was so frightened by the voice that he screamed and jumped to his left.

"Who's there?" Eli called as he scanned the tree to see if he could see who it was that spoke to him.

"It's me," said the voice again, though Eli could not see who was speaking.

"It's me who?" replied Eli, still searching for the source.

"It's me, you!" said the voice, this time coming from right behind Eli.

Eli turned and gasped as he looked into his own face. Standing behind Eli was Eli; only this other Eli did not have a body like Eli but rather had a transparent body that looked like it was formed from steam, almost like what Eli would imagine a ghost to look like.

"Are you a ghost?" asked Eli.

Eli knew that ghosts did not exist, at least not in the physical realm, but he was in the spirit realm now and he did not know if their existence was possible here.

"A ghost? No way!" The transparent Eli laughed. "I am you or you are me, or whatever. We are the same Eli. And I have got to say that I am very uncomfortable with the place that you have brought us."

"I don't understand," said Eli. "How can we be the same?"

The transparent Eli dismissed Eli's question by spreading his arms, inviting Eli to look around him.

"That's not what you need to be concerned with. This is the spirit realm and there are always going to be things that you don't fully understand. But one thing that you do understand is death, and this place reeks of death! Just look around you. The grass is dead, the trees are dead, and you will soon find out that the whole purpose of this place is to deal with the dead!"

"What do you mean the whole purpose of this place is to deal with the dead?" asked Eli.

"Why don't you walk up to the top of the hill and find out for yourself?" replied the transparent Eli.

Eli walked up the hill, careful to stay on the path of light. The two Elis did not talk as they walked, because Eli still thought it weird to have a conversation with himself, but Eli could hear the snide remarks of the transparent Eli as he documented all the ways that this place gave him the creeps.

"Eerie darkness; check. Bone chilling wind; check. Lots of dead stuff all around us; check."

Eli was just about to tell himself to be quiet when he reached the top of the hill and stood there in shock. The transparent Eli walked next to Eli and put his transparent arm around Eli's shoulders and said, "That is exactly what I am talking about."

Standing on top of the hill, flanked on both sides by a ten-foot-tall black cast-iron fence, with the path of light going directly under it, was the most terrifying gate Eli could have imagined. The gate was one large humanoid skull with its mouth open. The skull was not made out of iron, but bone, and Eli could not see how this could have been made except for the fact that the creature whose head now allowed passage down the path was once alive. The skull had only one eye socket centered above the nose and above that eye socket, carved directly into the bone, was the word,

CEMETERY.

The open mouth of the skull that formed the entrance had two rows of sharp canine teeth at least two-to-three-feet tall flanking the path. The skull looked as if it were in a perpetual state of roaring and the way the cold wind swept through the skull making a howling noise allowed Eli's imagination to think it was indeed howling at Eli.

"Please tell me that you are not seriously considering going into that place!" said the transparent Eli with his arm still around Eli's shoulders. "Because that would be the worst decision ever."

Eli thought for a moment before responding.

"Of course I am still going in there. It is obvious that the light path is telling me to go in that direction and so my mission for the King requires me to enter that gate."

Flinching a little when Eli mentioned the King, the transparent Eli countered, "But this is a cemetery! This is not a place that people go to fulfill missions. This is a place people go to die. I don't know why anyone would send you here on purpose. This has to be a mistake; you are not meant to be here. I say we go back to the gazebo, take the portal back to the atrium, and let them know that we are not willing to go through the most terrifying cemetery ever just to make them happy."

The transparent Eli's words appealed to Eli, but there was something wrong. Eli did not know for sure but something about this situation seemed fishy to him. As he thought about what seemed off, he could hear the words of Michael echoing in his mind.

"The only person keeping you from being a defender is you."

"This is the test," said Eli aloud yet quietly.

"What? What are you saying?" asked the transparent Eli.

"The test, you know, the one Michael was talking about back in the castle. The test that many possible defenders fail is to overcome themselves. When you say that you are me, what do you mean?"

Looking uncomfortable, the transparent Eli replied, "You know, we are the same. Just look at us, we are identical."

"No we aren't," said Eli. "In the spirit realm, I have a body and you don't."

"So what? What possible difference does that make?"

"You are not spiritual. You do not have a spirit and therefore you can't have a body here. That tells me that you are not part of me, who I really am, but that you are part of me, as in part of my earthly body. You are my flesh, aren't you?"

When Eli asked that question, two things happened: first, the transparent Eli's countenance changed from friendly to fierce; and second, more words appeared carved into the skull following the word CEMETERY,

...OF THE OLD MAN.

"You're my old man, my sinful flesh!" said Eli with an excitement that comes with solving a riddle.

"Oh wow," quipped Eli's flesh with a mean sarcasm in his voice. "Look who sounds like a goody-goody churchgoer now. I thought we were better than that. I thought we decided that all that Bible talk was just for losers. I thought we decided that it wasn't real."

"We were wrong," said Eli with a calm determination that made his flesh uncomfortable. "We have learned that the Bible is the King's Word and everything it teaches is truth. Further, we have learned that the King has called us to be the next defender of the realms and desires that we complete this mission, whatever it may be. Now I see that completing this first mission may include me defeating you."

"Oh you think so?" said Eli's flesh snidely.

"Yes I do and it seems obvious since we have come to the Cemetery of the Old Man that we have come to find you a new home."

"Oh really!" shouted Eli's flesh. "Well I am here to tell you that you don't have a chance at victory! I am stronger than you, smarter than you, and I know all about this place. If you dare enter this cemetery, I promise that it will not be me who finds a new home but you!"

"I don't think so," replied Eli calmly. "But I guess we are going to have to find out."

Eli's flesh contorted with rage and yelled out as a gust of bone-chilling wind swept across the hill picking him up and sending him through the gateway with such force that the skull again vibrated with the sound of a howl.

Eli took one last look around him and at the skull gate before walking in between the teeth of the skull and into the cemetery. Waiting on the other side of the gate was a floating envelope with his name written on it in his grandfather's handwriting. Excitedly, Eli grabbed the envelope, opened it, and pulled out the letter.

Elijah,

Welcome to the Cemetery of the Old Man. If you are reading this note, then you have already encountered your flesh and have decided to follow through with the King's mission. I am proud of you, Eli, but don't think that your flesh has given up or that the Enemy is not going to actively try to keep you from fulfilling this mission. This cemetery is an extremely dangerous place full of the Enemy's servants. If you are not careful, you will not make it to the end alive.

Fortunately, the King has left a way for you to be successful. The King has placed His protection upon the path you stand on now. Elijah, stay on the path! I don't care what you see or what you hear as you walk through the cemetery; do not leave this path. As long as you are on the path, you are safe. Also, make sure you keep the King's Word handy! You will find that it has the power to prevail when all else fails.

Continue on the path and it will lead you to where you must go. You will know that you have arrived when you see your name somewhere you would not want to see it.

Way beyond proud of you,
Grandpa

Eli finished reading the letter and was going to fold it up and keep it when the paper slowly faded away until nothing was left. Eli looked at his empty hands for a moment and then noticed the path his grandfather had told him about. There was nothing fancy about this path; it looked like a simple dirt path that had been cleared of all grass and stone that cut through the cemetery. As soon as the letter disappeared, a bright light illumined the path making it stand out in the dark surroundings.

"Stay on the path. That should not be so hard. Thanks, Grandpa, for the advice."

As he walked, Eli realized that he had only been to a cemetery twice, once for his grandmother's funeral and once for his grandfather's funeral. The cemetery his grandparents were buried in was a small, quiet, and pleasant little country church cemetery. The cemetery he was walking through right now was anything but small, pleasant, and quiet.

Eli could not see how big the cemetery was because of a dense fog that seemed to ascend upon the cemetery the moment he walked through the skull, but from what he saw on the top of the hill, he knew it must stretch for miles. As for the pleasant aspect, this cemetery was the opposite of pleasant. The landscape Eli could see was horrifying. There were countless sections of tombstones separated by black cast iron fences, many of these fences had been broken apart, pulled up, or demolished in some way. Eli was not sure what could bend and twist the iron like it was but he was sure that he did not want to think about it. The cemetery also had more dead trees strewn randomly across the different sections, each one looking as if it had been burned and had its limbs sharpened to razor points. Further, there were many gravestones that were destroyed, or that appeared to be burned. If that was not bad enough, Eli noticed that a lot of the graves had also been dug up and now lay empty with no sign of their former occupants.

But of all the elements of the cemetery that bothered Eli the most, it was the noises. The cold air rang with the echoes of rage-filled screams, deep rumbling growls, and loud clicking noises Eli could not identify.

Well isn't this a lovely place, thought Eli.

"No it isn't, and it only gets worse," said another voice to Eli's right.

Turning quickly to see where the voice came from, Eli was again face to face with his flesh.

"What are you doing back?" asked Eli. "I thought I told you that I am going to fulfill my mission for the King."

"You did," responded Eli's flesh in a nonchalant tone. "But I am here to warn you about what you are walking into. You see, this cemetery knows you Eli, it actually knows you. It knows your fears and your weaknesses. Everything that you fear can come to fruition here. Listen, it is your choice to continue on, but I am warning you that what lies ahead of you is going to be worse than any nightmare you have ever had. So, go on if you want, but don't come crying to me when you find yourself destroyed in this realm by the things you fear most."

Before Eli could respond, Eli's flesh smiled and evaporated into thin air. Wanting to show his flesh and the cemetery that he was not afraid, Eli called out into the cold darkness, "It doesn't matter. I am not afraid. I will complete my mission for the King."

Eli felt the ground underneath him rumble as if the cemetery was laughing at him. Drawing courage from what he felt was a direct challenge by the cemetery and his flesh, Eli walked determinedly down the path and into the heart of the cemetery.

chapter 13
the plot of forgetfulness

Walking down the path, Eli could not shake the feeling that he was being watched. This feeling made Eli nervous because he did not feel so much that he was being watched by something or someone in the cemetery, but rather, the cemetery itself was watching him and aware of his movements. Because of this feeling, Eli translated every gush of cold wind as a challenge to his resolve and every noise in the darkness as a means to intimidate him. It did not help Eli's resolve that the noises that used to be so distant now seemed to be drawing closer and closer.

Eli was on high alert when he saw it, out of the corner of his eye, a wisp of movement. Turning quickly on his heels, Eli looked to see what horrendous creature of the dark was about to storm him and do battle. But what Eli saw was not some creature, but rather an old friend from elementary school walking in the darkness. As Eli watched this friend walk, his old art classroom appeared out of nowhere and suddenly she was walking from the teacher's desk back to her art table where Eli was sitting with one of his friends.

"Ah, yes," came the voice of Eli's flesh from beside him. "I thought this memory might come up."

Not turning to look at him, Eli responded, "How is this possible? How are we watching this happen here? I don't understand."

"Did I not warn you?" asked Eli's flesh. "This cemetery knows you Eli. It knows all of your memories, and in this case, your greatest regrets. You and I both know what is about to happen. You are about to be dared to push her chair out from under her by Blake."

"Yes," replied Eli, "and then I called her a beached whale when she was lying on the floor."

"That's right," said Eli's flesh. "And she never forgave you for that."

"So why am I seeing this now?" asked Eli.

"You are seeing this now because this is the one place that you can make this regret right. You see, this is a special place called the plot of forgetfulness. This is a special place because it offers you a one-time opportunity to literally bury the memory of your choice. In your case, this terrible act of meanness that you have never forgiven yourself for can disappear never to haunt you again."

"Really?" asked Eli. "What's the catch? What is it going to cost me to have that done?"

"Cost you?" replied Eli's flesh in a hurt tone. "It isn't going to cost you anything. All you have to do is take that golden box that contains this memory and throw it in the open grave. Once that is done, the memory will disappear and never haunt you again."

Eli watched the memory play out as his flesh explained the process of burying the memory. Sure enough, after the memory played out and the girl ran off crying, a golden box appeared next to an open grave. Instantly, a deep longing sprung up inside of Eli to have that memory erased from his mind.

"Promise me that you are not lying," said Eli to his flesh.

"I am not lying," replied Eli's flesh. "I am not saying that I am not a liar. We both know that I am, but in this case, I don't have to lie to you. If you take that box and place it in the grave the memory will never bother you again. That is the truth."

Eli's flesh walked off the path and over to the golden box. Trying to pick it up but having his arms pass through it like steam, Eli's flesh called out, "I would totally do it for you, but as you can see, my physical body is unable to pick it up in the spirit realm. If you want this memory gone, you are going to have to do it yourself."

Eli looked down at the path and then to where the box lay as another path appeared that led from where Eli was standing to the box. This other path was not lit like the one he was on and it was not clear of debris either, having a large pile of dead leaves on the left side of the path just a few short steps onto the path.

Eli could hear the words from the letter echoing in his mind to stay on the path, but Eli's desire to rid himself of that memory was telling him to go after that box. Eli's desire to bury that box was so strong, it almost felt as if the cemetery itself was urging Eli to go and bury the box.

Eli took a step toward the other path when he saw it, a small movement under the pile of leaves and a millisecond reflection of light. Eli froze, feeling as if he knew what he just saw but could not remember. Eli's flesh saw the hesitation in Eli and once again encouraged Eli to get rid of that memory once and for all. When Eli was just about to take the next step off the path and onto the other path, a brief memory stopped him in his tracks.

Eli was out one night with his grandfather and his grandfather was going to show him a trick. Eli's grandfather knew that Eli was afraid of spiders and so he was going to show Eli how to see if spiders were in the grass. They both had flashlights and they placed them on the tip of their noses and shined them in the grass. If a spider was in the grass, the light would reflect off its eyes giving away its position.

Knowing that Eli had just seen what he thought was a very large reflection of light come from the bottom of the pile of leaves caused Eli to back up very slowly.

"What's the matter with you?" called Eli's flesh. "Don't you want to be rid of that terrible memory?"

"Yes I do," called Eli as he acted like he was going to walk off the lit path but stopped right before stepping onto the other path. About the time Eli's foot would have hit the other path, the pile of leaves flew up and a giant trap-door-spider flung its hairy legs onto the path expecting to grab hold of its prey. When it realized Eli was out of reach, it barred its large fangs that were dripping with poison and made a loud and terrifying hissing noise before retreating back into its lair.

Hearing his flesh let out a cry of disappointment, Eli yelled, "You lied to me! You wanted that thing to get me! How could you? Why would you want us to be devoured by a giant spider?"

"First," said Eli's flesh, "I did not lie to you. If you would have come out here, that memory would not bother you anymore. I wager you would have had bigger things on your mind. Second, you act like we are friends and yet you have come to the Cemetery of the Old Man to put an end to me. What did you expect me to do? I just want what you want and that is to live. So I will make you a deal: turn around and allow us to go back to being one and the same and I will not lead you into any other dangers."

"Not a chance!" growled Eli as he turned his back on his flesh and stormed down the path to the sound of his flesh's mocking laughter.

chapter 14
the devourers

Eli stormed down the path with a renewed zeal spurred on by his flesh's attempt to destroy him. Zoning out the noises and the increasingly strong gushes of wind, Eli was determined to walk briskly down the path without stopping until he came to the end. The attempt on Eli's life convinced Eli of two things: the stakes in the cemetery were high, and the path truly offered protection from anything and everything lurking in the cemetery.

Eli walked down the path through a section of the cemetery that looked as if it belonged to one of the earliest eras in human history. There were no gravestones marking underground graves, but instead the landscape was dotted with small caves. The caves looked identical with each cave having a small opening covered with a large stone.

The tops of these caves seemed to be moving but the more Eli looked at them he realized that the movement was being caused by a mixture of light and shadow dancing on the tops of the caves. The further Eli walked the more dominant the shadows became until he topped a hill and saw the source of the dancing light.

The light originated from a large cave that was identical to the other caves with the difference being that this cave was at least ten times as large and the gigantic opening to the cave had no stone covering it. This cave was located on the left side of the path about halfway between the path and the horizon, and had a path that looked identical to the path that Eli was now walking on leading directly into the cave's mouth. Inside the cave Eli saw a large roaring fire with a wooden rotisserie slowly cooking a chunk of meat.

Though Eli did not like the look of the cave, the fire, or the fact that a path that looked identical to the path he was walking on led to the cave's mouth, it was the gigantic hand turning the rotisserie that demanded Eli's attention. The hand was humanoid, but Eli knew it did not belong to a human. This hand was so large Eli knew his whole body could easily fit into the hand with room to spare. Covering this hand was a thick leathery skin covered in scars and thick black hair. The fingers that grasped and turned the rotisserie were long and crooked and had long talon-like fingernails that were filthily covered with what looked like a mixture of blood and dirt.

Eli stood still, not moving and barely breathing, hoping that whatever was in that cave would not notice his presence. Cautiously, Eli continued his walk down the path when a grizzly rumble resonated out of the darkness. Frozen in place, Eli realized this hair-raising rumble was the creature's laughter.

"Well, well, well, look what we have here!" The grizzly voice laughed. "I don't remember ordering delivery, but I will eat it all the same!"

The creature's grizzly laugh echoed off the walls of the cave and silenced all the other noises of the cemetery.

"And its color band is so pretty. I don't think we have a silver one yet."

At that moment, the hand that was turning the rotisserie shook, causing a large number of different colored bracelets to slide down on to the wrist of the creature. Horrified, Eli realized that the creature's bracelets were made from the colored stripes that spanned from the right shoulder to the left hip on the defender uniform.

"Why don't you just come and face me now, defender, like a true warrior? One way or another, you will come to my cave. It is better for you to come and die with dignity rather than screaming and begging for mercy!"

Once again the creature laughed, but this time the laugh was filled with a terrifying madness that scared Eli so bad he took off running down the path. As Eli ran, he tried to get the picture of the hand out of his mind. Knowing what the creature wore for bracelets only allowed Eli to think of one thing the creature could be cooking over the fire: former defenders.

But how could the creature get the defenders if they were on the path? thought Eli as he slowed to a walk again. "Grandpa said the path is safe. But there was a path that led to the cave and it was identical to the path I am walking on now!"

That thought forced Eli to stop walking and to examine the path he was on.

"Light!" exclaimed Eli. "This path is a path of light. The other path did not have light. As long as I stay on the path that is lit I should never go toward that horrific cave."

Eli continued his trek down the path as the surroundings changed from the landscape of small caves to a landscape of crumbling stone headstones and scary-looking dead trees. The cold wind gushed through the cemetery once again and Eli noticed the treetops were wrapped with what looked like cotton thread that waved in the wind. The deeper into this section of the cemetery Eli walked, the more prevalent this cotton thread was found in the trees. Before long, entire trees and many of the gravestones were completely wrapped with this thick white thread.

Something else bothered Eli as he walked through this section, but he could not identify what it was until he heard a loud clicking noise that startled him. It was then that he realized all the noises of the cemetery that had been present from the beginning of his walk were now almost completely gone. This part of the cemetery was completely silent save for a loud clicking noise that echoed through the trees at random times. This clicking noise seemed odd to Eli because it sounded like someone was typing on a large, old-fashioned typewriter. The clicking grew louder the further Eli walked but stopped suddenly as Eli walked around a bend in the road.

Eli almost did not notice the silence because of the giant funnel of white thread lying on the ground on the right side of the path perfectly between the path and the horizon. The funnel was huge and looked like a massive tornado frozen in time lying on its side. Leading into the mouth of the funnel was a path, which like the path that led directly into the cave with the giant, was identical to the path Eli was walking on now without the light.

After standing in awe of the scene for a moment, the loud clicking noise began again, and this time, Eli could tell that it was resonating from inside the large funnel. Eli could see movement inside the funnel and saw what looked like a dark shadow rapidly shoot from the thin part of the funnel in the back to the entrance of the tunnel at incredible speed.

Audibly gasping in terror, Eli felt as if his worst nightmare was about to take place as a giant spider spilled out of the entrance of the funnel. The spider was black and hairy with a white and black design covering its back. The spider had multiple eyes, each one solid black, but Eli knew that each one was fixed on him. The loud clicking noise came from the spider's massive pinchers that were dripping with saliva or poison, Eli did not know which.

As the spider regarded Eli, Eli heard its voice that sounded like a mix between hissing and whispering.

"Welcome, defender. I was wondering when my next meal would arrive. Look at you! So young and tender, and such a nice outfit! Your suit will look amazing in my collection!"

The giant spider laughed and lifted one of its massive legs pointing to a row of trees not far from the side of the funnel. Hanging in these trees by threads of webbing, were whole suits of clothing like the one Eli was wearing from the castle like ornaments on a Christmas tree. Eli did not feel like counting but he saw several suits on each tree and there were several rows of decorated trees.

As if the spider could read Eli's thoughts, it continued its verbal assault.

"Oh yes, you too will make a nice addition to my garden. I await your steps on my path."

Terrified, Eli could not muster anything more than a shake of his head as if to say no. Noticing his terror, the spider charged toward Eli with lightning speed and stopped just inches from the boundary of the path.

Seeing the giant spider up close made Eli feel faint. The legs of the spider were taller than Eli and the spider's body was easily two to three times larger than Eli's body. Eli knew that he was now looking up at a spider that would have no problem capturing, killing, and eating him. Staring at the giant spider's pinchers dripping and clicking so close to him caused Eli to physically shake with fear.

"What's the matter, defender?" hissed the spider. "Are you afraid? You ought to be afraid. If you continue down the path you will see me again and when you do, you will not have the protection of the path to keep you from me."

As the spider spoke, it reached one of its hairy legs up and touched the path directly in front of Eli's face. The air around the path shimmered and the spider's leg received a shock that made the spider recoil with a painful hiss.

"Soon, defender. Soon I will devour you and hang your clothes in my garden."

The spider sped back into its funnel with a terrifying hissing laughter. Eli turned and continued walking, making sure that he was squarely in the center of the path.

The spider webs slowly disappeared as Eli entered a new section of the cemetery. The landscape of dead trees covered with nasty spider webs gave way to a tree-less landscape of uniform graves and a horizon of eerie darkness. The gravestones were all made of white stone and all were identical in perfectly symmetrical rows. It reminded Eli of the time he visited Arlington Cemetery in Washington D.C.

Eli decided that he was only going to focus on the path ahead of him instead of trying to understand everything that was surrounding his path. After a few moments of walking down that path, Eli heard a noise that he did not ever think he would hear in a place like this: laughter.

Laughter echoed off the gravestones and pierced the eerie darkness surrounding Eli. This laughter did not lift Eli's spirits but rather put Eli on edge. The laughter was not only out of place in this creepy land, but it was strangely familiar to Eli. By the time Eli reached the top of a hill from which he knew the laughter was coming, he was not surprised to see the two people whose laughter he knew: his grandfather and himself.

There at the top of the hill on a plateau was Eli's flesh, what he guessed what his grandfather's flesh, and two skeletons, one with large green eyes and one with large blue eyes, sitting around a poker table playing cards and laughing. The table was located just off the path to the left; however, where their table sat on the ground, the lit path broke off into three identical paths, none of which, to Eli's terror, had the light of the path that Eli was walking on.

chapter 15
a choice with a high chance of death

Impossible! thought Eli. *This can't be happening! Where is the path with the light?*

The images of the paths leading into the lairs of the monsters he had encountered on the road filled Eli's mind with dread. Eli did not even try to hide the fear he felt when the group at the poker table took notice of him.

"Hey, buddy! Wow, it is good to see you again!" called out Eli's grandfather's flesh. "After being buried in this place I did not ever think I would see you again. Man, Eli, you don't look so good. Are you okay?"

At that moment, Eli's flesh put down his cards. "Read 'em and weep, boys. Looks like I win again!"

The skeletons and Eli's grandfather's flesh all threw their cards down laughing and joking with each other.

Eli did not have to guess why the cemetery created this scene for him because the longing inside of him to join them at the table and spend time with any part of his grandfather, even if it was his flesh, was already threatening to overwhelm his determination to continue on. Coupled with the fear of the disappearing light from the path, this last scene was more than enough to make Eli want to give up altogether.

"See what I mean?" said Eli's flesh to his grandfather's flesh. "He is not the same person he used to be. It's like he doesn't even know who we are anymore. I think now that he has gone all Christian and all that he is too good for us. I mean look at him, he won't even talk to you after not seeing you for so long."

"Is that true, Eli?" asked his grandfather's flesh in a hurt tone. "Are you just going to stand there and ignore me as if you are too good for me now? Don't you recognize me? Don't you remember all the good times we had together?"

"No. I mean yes, I do recognize you, and I do remember times we had around a table like that," said Eli as he slowly recovered from the shock of the disappearing light on the paths. "But that is not who I am anymore and that is not who you are anymore."

"Not who I am anymore?" repeated Eli's grandfather's flesh slowly, as if trying to digest each word. "What are you saying, Eli, that I am not your grandpa who you used to spend so much time with? Are you saying that I am not one of your best friends and one of the people who know you better than anyone else?"

"What I mean," said Eli with an increasing confidence that was fueled by an inner anger at the cemetery's latest attempt to discourage and distract him, "is that you are the person that I used to hold higher than anyone else and the person with whom I used to enjoy talking and joking about things that I am now ashamed to think about; but now, the grandpa I know and love is the grandpa who buried you here for good reason. Now I hold the King higher than anyone else and seeing you here does make me sad, not to relive those days, but because I know that you are here to get me to quit. You are here to get me to do something that is harmful to me and something that is not good for me. I am sad because I see now that if you truly loved me, the way that the grandpa that buried you here loves me, then you would not be attempting to hinder me."

Eli's flesh and the two skeletons laughed mockingly at Eli as his grandfather's flesh replied, "You think I am trying to hinder you? Do you not see what is before you? There are three paths here and two of them lead to this cemetery's devourers. You know who I am speaking of; I am sure you saw them before you arrived here. One is large, angry, and very good at crushing the bones of defenders with his bare hands. The other is nasty, black, and likes to drink little defenders out of their clothes. Ten steps down each of these paths is a little portal that will transport you to one of three paths and then will immediately seal itself. One portal takes you to the mouth of a cave, one takes you to the mouth of a funnel web, and one leads you to the end of this path. Not only has *your* King allowed for these other paths to be here, but He has also allowed for His light that has led you this far to end right here at the most important crossroads in the cemetery. So tell me who is trying to hinder you, who is trying to hurt you, and who is trying to help you?

All the fear and confusion Eli felt when he first arrived at the crossroads swelled up again. Eli's face must have communicated this fear because his grandfather's flesh wasted no time in pointing it out.

"I can see the fear in your eyes, Eli, and to be honest with you, you ought to be afraid. You say I am trying to hurt you or hinder you, but in reality, I am trying to offer you a path that does not have a high percentage chance of leading to a terrible death. You can either stay here with us and we will pull you up a chair or you can turn around and go down the path that you know is protected and exit this cemetery before you earn yourself a grave here. Listen, we did not have to come here. We could have just let you pick a path without knowing the possible consequences and allowed you to make a decision that has a two-out-of-three chance of leading to your death. Tell me, buddy, who is working for your harm: me or your King? Which path will you take: the one that could destroy you or the one you know is safe?"

Eli was speechless. All he could see were the identical paths in front of the cave and the web, and all he could hear was the grizzly laughter of the giant mixed with the hissing laughter of the spider. The words of Eli's grandfather's flesh rang in Eli's ears as he wondered why the King would allow a situation like this. But even with his doubts and fears, Eli felt as if he was missing something that he needed to figure out.

Eli knew that the King would not leave him stranded without a way to know which path was the safe path. However, Eli also knew that it looked like many other defenders had made the wrong choice when it came to the path they took. As Eli thought about what the King would desire him to do, he noticed something odd about the skeletons sitting around the table. Both of the skeletons were nothing more than bone except for their eyes: they each had large round eyes. The blue and the green of their irises made for a striking contrast with their ghostly white bones which might have been why their eye movement caught Eli's attention. Eli noticed that they both kept looking at his face and then they would take quick glances down to his waist. Curious, Eli looked down and noticed that the pages of his Bible were glowing faintly. Eli reached down and took his Bible out of its sheaf and felt the Bible attempting to connect with his mind. Eli closed his eyes and concentrated. Soon a verse popped into his mind and before he knew it he was reciting the verse quietly.

"And Jesus said unto him, 'No man, having put his hand to the plough, and looking back, is fit for the kingdom of God.'"

"What was that?" called Eli's grandfather's flesh.

"I said that no man having put his hand to the plough, and looking back, is fit for the kingdom of God," said Eli. "It means that I am not going back and I am not going to quit just because there is a chance I might die."

Eli felt a wave of strength and confidence flow through him as he quoted the King's Word and chose to heed it.

"I am going to go on for the King and complete His mission," continued Eli, fueled by this new confidence.

"Then you will be able to keep having so much fun with my flesh after I bury him here forever."

"You were always a smart-mouth," quipped his grandfather's flesh. "Tell me then, defender Eli, which path will you choose?"

"You have got to be kidding me!" called out Eli's flesh. "Only a fool would take his chances with such a terrible death on the line! But, if you are going to insist on killing us, at least tell me that you are going to use your brain when deciding our fate. It should be obvious, take the middle path. If the spider was on the right and the creature was on the left, then just take the middle path."

"I am not going to take any path!" began Eli.

"What are you talking about?" interrupted Eli's flesh before he was cut off.

"Until I have consulted the King's Word," finished Eli.

Eli concentrated and once again the King's Word filled his thoughts.

"There is a way that seems right to a man, but the ends thereof are the ways of death," said Eli. "The middle path does seem to be the most logical, but the King's Word tells me that I cannot trust my own judgment."

"Well awesome!" shouted a flabbergasted Eli's flesh. "So what does the King's Word say about choosing a path if you cannot use your own reasoning and logic? Wait, let me guess: the King wants you to play rock, paper, scissors to pick a path?"

The skeletons and Eli's grandfather's flesh all burst out in mocking laughter but Eli was not deterred. Something happened to Eli every time he connected to the King's

Word. A power filled him, giving him more confidence and strength. Knowing the only way to find the right path lay in the King's Word, Eli concentrated on the Word and asked which path to take. After a brief moment, Eli felt a rush of energy and comfort as another passage filled his mind. With his eyes closed to his adversaries, Eli quoted the passage.

"Trust in the Lord with all your heart and lean not unto your own understanding. In all your ways acknowledge Him and He shall direct your steps."

Eli felt a gush of wind, but this time it was not a cold wind but a warm summer breeze. Opening his eyes he saw his grandfather's flesh and his flesh as well as the table and two of the three paths blow away in the wind as if they were dust particles. When the wind ceased, all that remained were two skeletons giving him a very threatening look as if to say, "This is not over boy!" and one path: the path on the left. With the other two paths gone, the path on the left extended back and connected with the path Eli was standing on. The light from the path that led Eli to this point extended down the remaining path, lighting Eli's way once again.

Eli walked past the skeletons and after taking ten steps he was immediately transported to the end of the path. Eli knew it was the end of the path because standing before him at the end of the path was a large mausoleum with his name etched into it.

"That is definitely not the place I want to see my name, so this must be the end of the path!" said Eli as he looked at the structure.

"Oh, this is the end, defender!" snarled a terrifyingly familiar voice from behind Eli.

Eli shot around and saw the Enemy in his giant lion form standing just inches from the path's border right behind Eli.

"Your end!" yelled the Enemy and he lunged for Eli.

chapter 16
the enemy's assault

The giant lion flew through the air and hit the protective barrier with all of his might. The barrier prevented the Enemy from reaching Eli, but the Enemy continued his assault by repeatedly pounding the barrier with his massive paws. Momentarily stopping his assault, the Enemy roared an ear-splitting, terrifying roar filled with both the Enemy's desire to kill Eli and his determination to destroy the barrier. Instinctively Eli backed up from the assault with his eyes fixed on the massive lion creature working desperately to get a hold of him. Not thinking about what was behind him, Eli kept backing up until he placed the heel of his right foot off of the path.

This must have been what the Enemy had planned because immediately skeletal hands shot out of the ground and grabbed Eli's heel and pulled it out from under him causing Eli to fall on his stomach.

"Pull him off the path and hold him!" yelled the Enemy.

Eli looked up and saw the giant lion creature run toward the mausoleum and Eli figured he only had a few moments before the Enemy made it around the mausoleum and down the other side of the path to where Eli was now being dragged. Eli flipped himself over to see what was dragging him off the path. Eli's glance was met by two large sets of eyes, one with green irises and one with blue irises. Briefly taken aback by the sudden appearance of the skeletons he thought he had left behind at the crossroads, Eli quickly recovered and began his attempt to free himself.

Eli thrashed his legs wildly in an attempt to free them from the grips of the skeletons, but the bony grip of the skeletons was surprisingly strong. Feeling himself pulled further off the path and seeing the Enemy rounding the mausoleum in his peripheral vision, Eli knew that he had to do something fast. Eli scanned the path for any rock, stick, or weapon he could use but did not see anything. The only action Eli could think to take was to reach for his Bible. Eli reached his hand to his side and grabbed the Bible but he dropped it as the skeletons' attempt to get Eli off the path became more violent. When the Bible hit the ground, a bright flash of light momentarily exploded from the pages. The light seemed to burn the skeleton's eyes and they were forced to let go of Eli to cover their eyes. Taking advantage of that moment, Eli kicked one of the skeletons in the head, sending his head rolling away into the darkness. With one skeleton chasing his head and the other skeleton still recovering from the burst of light, Eli was able to pull both his legs back onto the path.

"No!" shouted the Enemy in a long and rage-filled roar as he had arrived and only missed his prey by a few seconds.

The Enemy unleashed his fury against the skeletons by hitting them with his paws, sending their bones soaring into the air like dead leaves in a breeze. Satisfied with his dismantling of the skeletons for their failure, the large lion walked to the very edge of the path, licked his large yellow teeth, and glared at Eli from a sitting position.

Eli lay on his back for a moment before sitting up and placing his Bible back into its sheaf. Slowly and cautiously, Eli stood up, brushed himself off and walked toward the mausoleum without looking back at the Enemy.

The mausoleum looked like an elevator. It was about eight feet tall, and four feet wide with what looked to be elevator doors facing Eli. The outside of the mausoleum was completely reflective giving it the appearance of a large mirror. Elijah's full name was etched in his own messy handwriting with gold inlay just above the elevator looking door. Receiving a rush of confidence, knowing that his trek through the cemetery was over, Eli walked toward the mausoleum.

"I would not go in there if I were you," said a voice that seemed much smoother and more human-like than what Eli expected from the lion.

"Oh really?" said Eli as he turned to confront the Enemy. "And why not?" asked Eli as his voice trailed off in shocked silence.

Sitting where the lion was sitting just a moment ago was a handsome man who resembled Michael in a lot of ways. The Enemy looked identical to Michael in height and build and could easily pass for Michael's twin if it were not for a few key differences. Instead of golden blonde hair, the Enemy's hair was ink black like the darkness that engulfed the cemetery. Instead of white robes and a golden breastplate, the Enemy covered his entire body with form-fitting black armor. The Enemy's supernatural physique coupled with the black armor reminded Eli of a giant-sized Batman. The Enemy's eyes also caught Eli's attention because they were solid black. The Enemy's countenance seemed to radiate darkness the same way Michael's countenance radiated light. The Enemy sat on a throne that looked like it had been formed from the bones of the skeletons he just dismantled a few moments ago as a lion. Despite the throne and the black armor, this man exuded a sense of invitation and comradery that Eli felt difficult to resist. In the same way that Michael made Eli feel safe, the Enemy made Eli feel like his friend.

"Why would you not go in there?" said Eli, trying to regain his composure.

"Because that is a tomb, Eli, and it has your name on it. I commend you on how bravely you have fought to stay alive and conquer this cemetery, and I just don't think you would be willing to throw your life away by walking into your own grave."

"That is a tomb," replied Eli, trying not to allow the Enemy's compliment to soften his resolve. "And that is my name on the tomb; however, I know that if I enter that tomb, I won't be throwing my life away."

"And how could you possibly know that?" enquired the Enemy in a gentle and smooth tone of voice.

"I know that because my King has brought me here, not to die, but to live and become a defender in His service."

"No, no, no, you poor thing," began the Enemy with deep compassion filling his voice. "Eli, the King has deceived you, just as He has deceived so many other people before you. Don't you think the defenders who found their way into the cave of the giant or the web of the spider thought the King had brought them here to live? Son, if I can call you that, the King doesn't want you to live. He wants you to die. Why else would He have brought you to a cemetery and have a mausoleum with your name on it?"

The power of the Enemy's words and his ability to make Eli feel like his friend were rapidly wearing down Eli's resolve to go into that mausoleum. For the first time since Eli entered the cemetery, he actually contemplated turning around and going back. Seeing his opportunity, the Enemy continued his assault.

"I know this must be hard for you to grasp, but believe me I understand. I used to minister to the King. In fact, I was His most loyal and trustworthy minister. Then one day, I saw Him for who He really was. And when I made a stand for what is right, Eli, He cast me and all those who wanted to stand for what is right out of His presence. The pain I suffered at the hands of your King is the motivation behind what I am doing. Eli, I don't want you to suffer the same pain and so I have done everything I can to keep you from being deceived. Please Eli, don't make the mistake I made and trust the King. He is not worthy of your life."

Thinking he had successfully persuaded Eli, the Enemy leaned forward and extended his hand for Eli to take. But Eli was not persuaded. In fact, the Enemy had unknowingly rekindled Eli's love for the King and hate for the Enemy. When the Enemy mentioned his being cast out of the King's presence, Eli's mind went back to his conversation with Zephyr in the castle and Eli remembered seeing the great pain on Zephyr's and Brutus' face as they remembered the treachery. Eli then thought about the fall of man because of the Enemy, and all the terrible deaths, diseases, and other effects of sin throughout history. Even though the Enemy's power over words and emotions was strong, the devastation his work had wrought reminded Eli of his true nature.

"You are pathetic," growled Eli to the surprise of the Enemy. "You are the one who betrayed the King. You are the one who hurt the King, and you are the one who is responsible for all the pain and suffering in all of creation. And yet, you are going to sit here and blaspheme the name of my God who in His great mercy has allowed you to live!"

The Enemy rose to His feet as dark energy radiated from his countenance. "Mercy? You think I have my freedom because of His mercy? Don't make me laugh! I have my freedom and power because your King knows He cannot defeat me! That is the whole reason why He wants you to enter that tomb and die for Him. He thinks that your pathetic sacrifice will allow Him to defeat me. But He will never defeat me!"

"You are lying to yourself, and you know it," said Eli. "The King has the power to defeat you whenever He chooses. The only way for you to deny this is to ignore the obvious."

"Is that so?" mocked the Enemy. "Please enlighten me about the obvious facts I am ignoring."

"Gladly," spoke Eli with confidence. "You tried your best to kill me when I first arrived in the spirit realm and yet the King's light sent you running away. His light, not His army or His power. Merely the light from His throne room sent you running away into the darkness. Then, you sent my flesh and several of your minions to keep me from reaching the mausoleum; yet here I am because the power of the King's Word overrules all your traps. Just a few moments ago you again tried to kill me personally, but you are hindered by the power of the King's protection on the path. If you cannot overcome the mere light of the King and the simple protection the King has placed on this path, you are only lying to yourself by thinking you even have a chance to defeat the King."

The Enemy's countenance flashed again with darkness. "You are a fool, Elijah Storm, and one day you will regret these words. That is," said the Enemy as he regained a calm composure. "Unless you choose to listen to me now and abort this mission before it is too late. We admittedly disagree on some things, but as of now, you are not my enemy. If you choose to enter that mausoleum, you forever will become my enemy and I will use everything in my power to destroy you. But, if you turn around and go back the way you came, I promise I will leave you alone and never bother you again. What is it going to be Eli; do you really want me for an enemy?"

Eli turned and looked at the mausoleum as if he were contemplating the offer, but was really reaching down to grab his Bible without the Enemy seeing him. Holding his Bible, Eli closed his eyes and concentrated, seeking for the answer he needed to end this conversation and communicate that Eli was the property of the King, not the Enemy.

"Well, what is your choice?" asked the Enemy.

"I think," said Eli as he turned with his Bible in his hand, smiling at the Enemy. "It is time for you to run away like the coward you are."

The Enemy erupted with dark energy that seemed to radiate from his body as if he were on fire with pure black flames.

"What did you say to me?" yelled the Enemy, not hiding his rage.

"I said that it is time for you to run away like the coward you are," yelled Eli. "The King's Word says, 'Submit yourself unto God, resist the devil and he will flee from you.' I have submitted to the King. I have resisted your words and your offer and now, according to the Word that binds all creation, it is time for you to do your thing and run away."

"But —"

"NOW!" shouted Eli.

The Enemy glared at Eli before disappearing in a burst of darkness that looked like a puddle of ink being sucked into a black hole.

With the Enemy gone, Eli returned his Bible to its sheaf, and confidently approached the mausoleum. The doors slid open inviting Eli to enter. Eli could hardly believe it, he had completed his quest through the Cemetery of the Old Man. He had successfully avoided the traps of his flesh and the grips of the devourers. Moments ago, through the power of the King's Word, Eli had withstood the Enemy's words and sent him away. If all of that was not enough for one day, Eli was about to walk into a mausoleum with his name on it.

As Eli approached the mausoleum, he hesitated. *It does feel a little creepy walking into a tomb with my name on it,* thought Eli. With that in mind, Eli walked through the doors and into his own tomb.

chapter 17
the mausoleum

Eli stepped into the mausoleum and the elevator doors closed behind him. When the doors shut, there was a moment of absolute darkness before a soft green light illuminated the room. The glow seemed to resonate from the walls of the room which were also reflective. For a brief moment nothing happened. Eli stood there looking around at his reflection when he heard a loud click and felt the room begin to descend like an elevator.

Although the descent began with a loud clicking noise, the actual descent of the elevator was so quiet, Eli would have wondered if the room was moving at all if not for the feeling in his stomach that told him he was falling.

After what Eli guessed was about thirty seconds, the elevator slowed down and came to a stop. When the elevator stopped moving completely, all of the green light shut off for a second before turning back on. When the lights came on, Eli was startled to see his flesh looking back at him in the reflection on the doors of the elevator.

"What do you want?" asked Eli, trying not to show his surprise.

"You know what I want," began his flesh. "But I'm not here to trick you or to try and get you killed. I am here to warn you about a real danger you are going to face."

"Oh really," retorted Eli. "What could be more dangerous than being eaten by a giant spider or crushed to death by a giant, well, a giant whatever that thing was?"

Eli's flesh smiled as if the memory of what he did to Eli in the cemetery was funny to him. "Yes, I tried to get you caught by the spider and I would have loved to see you crushed to death by the giant, but you escaped the cemetery without harm. Inside this mausoleum is a different story. Even if you successfully navigate the mausoleum, which you will not, you will not escape unharmed."

"What do you mean?" asked Eli.

"First, for you to finish this task and exit the mausoleum you are going to have to face enemies far more dangerous than you can ever imagine," replied Eli's flesh. "These enemies are the reason why so many potential defenders fail to complete this mission. So forgive me for having low self-image, but I don't see why you think you are any better than the many defenders who have failed. Further, to defeat these enemies will require a great deal of pain and suffering on your behalf. Even if you somehow pull off the impossible and finish this so-called mission of yours, you will only achieve that through life-altering pain. Win or lose, you will never be the same again! Tell me, is that a challenge you feel you are ready for?"

"My name is Elijah Storm," announced Eli in a loud and clear voice. "I am a child of the Great King. I have been saved and commissioned by the King to fulfill the task in front of me. Just since the time of my arrival in the spirit realm I have escaped from the jaws of the Enemy, I have succeeded in overcoming your own plans for my destruction, avoided the devourers of the cemetery, and faced down the Enemy one-on-one. Do you really think your pathetic little speech about pain is going to get me to run away and quit now?"

Eli continued, "If I were you, I would get comfortable here, because I am about to overcome this mausoleum and bury you here just like I just overcame your master."

"You really think you can overcome the Enemy with a small book and glowing words?" mocked Eli's flesh. "The only reason you are still alive is because you had the protection of the path. That protection does not exist anywhere else in the realm, by the way, but that is not important. What is important is that you understand that even if you are the one who walks out of this tomb, you will do so only by killing me. If you have not figured it out yet, you and I are intimately intertwined. For you to bury me here will cost you far more than you could ever imagine. Our intimate connection is exactly why so many defenders have failed to complete this training. You are about to enter into the greatest lose-lose situation in all creation. I am offering you a way to turn this lose-lose situation into a positive one. Look here."

Eli's flesh pointed to a spot next to the elevator door and a red button with an arrow pointing up appeared.

"If you don't want to die a terrible death or suffer through putting part of yourself through a terrible death, then hit this button. This elevator will turn into a portal and take you back to the atrium. I promise you."

"I have heard this before!" cut in Eli. "I told you before and I will tell you again, I am not going back! Now, step aside, or disappear; I am going to walk through those doors and finish my task from the King. I would appreciate it if I did not have to see you again. It is not that I don't love these little talks; it is just that time is wasting and I have wasted enough of my life listening to you. Now leave!"

Eli's flesh shrugged his shoulders and put his hands in the air. "Okay, boss, but don't say I didn't warn you."

The lights flickered again and when they came back on, Eli's flesh was gone. The elevator made a dinging noise announcing its arrival and the doors opened revealing a long square hallway lined with mirror tiles on the floor, walls, and ceiling. As if someone hit a switch, the glowing green light illuminated the hallway beginning at the elevator and spreading down the corridor illuminating a large, movie-theatre-like room at the end of the corridor.

Eli walked down the hallway, constantly glancing at his reflection making sure it was not his flesh, with the squeaking of his shoes on the glass floors the only noise penetrating the silence. When Eli entered the movie-theatre-like room, he heard what sounded like an old-time projector start up and saw on the wall he was facing an old-time film begin playing. The film, which was in black and white, without sound, and constantly had little glitches and spots show up, looked as if it were filmed back in the 1940s. Eli soon got over the distraction of the film when he saw what the film was showing. There was a Man, sitting on a large grassy hill surrounded by people. This Man captivated Eli, because though Eli had never seen him before, there was something so familiar about him. Eli was sure that he knew this Man and loved this Man, but Eli could not place where he had ever seen him before. As the Man spoke to the crowd—at least that was what Eli was assuming he was doing because there was no sound—the Man turned and looked right at Eli. Eli's heart burned inside him as the Man smiled and winked at Eli before turning back to the crowd and speaking to them.

The picture on the screen changed and now showed what looked like an ancient farmer. This man was wearing Middle-Eastern style robes, a hat with a wrap-around large wavy brim, and a satchel with a strap that wrapped around the left shoulder of the man and rested on his right hip. This farmer reached into his satchel and pulled out a handful of seed. The farmer walked up and down his field tossing the seed everywhere he went. When he was finished, the camera shifted from the farmer and focused on the field.

Eli jumped back as a terrifying, black, crow-looking bird swooped out of the air and began devouring the seeds by the mouthful. Eli felt a shiver go down his spine as the bird looked up at Eli as if the bird could see him. The crow then smiled in such a way that made Eli feel that he could be the next thing the bird ate. With a mouth full of seed, the bird flew away.

The camera then focused on another group of seeds and Eli watched what appeared as a time lapse segment of film in which the seeds sank into the ground and began sprouting. Soon though, the sun began to bear down on the seeds and Eli watched as the little sprouts burst into flame and disintegrated.

Another group of seeds came into focus and again, time lapsed as the seeds sank into the ground and sprung up. This time, however, large nasty looking thorns sprung up from the ground, wrapped around the sprouts and dragged them down back into the soil.

Another group of seeds came into focus and again, a time lapse video showed the seeds sinking into the ground and sprouting up. This time, however, the sprouts grew up, became large healthy stalks of wheat, and produced large quantities for the farmer who harvested them.

The screen then went to a zoomed-in picture of the Man who was speaking to the crowd, only this time, the Man was talking directly to Eli. The Man smiled, and once again, Eli felt his spirit burn. The Man spoke, but instead of hearing the words through a speaker, Eli felt the voice of the Man resonate in his mind.

"My child, the seed that the farmer sows is the Word. You have heard the Word and you have received the Word. My desire for your life is that you become a great defender and produce much fruit; however, the path to produce fruit is not an easy one. You must show that you are ready to become a defender. In order to do this you must overcome and defeat the four enemies who will stop at nothing to prevent you from taking your place among the ranks of the defenders: the world, your earthly desires, the Enemy, and your flesh.

"In a moment you will be given a key. That key unlocks the first of four rooms that you must pass through in order to exit this mausoleum. The key to the next door will be found inside the room. For you to move on and overcome, you must battle each room and retrieve the key. I have overcome all of these enemies and have given you everything you need to be successful, but you must personally gain the victories over these enemies. My desire is for you to gain the victory and take your place among the great defenders of the realms. For you to achieve this, you must first survive your own funeral. I love you, my child, and am eager to welcome you when you gain the victory."

The projector noise ceased and the far wall returned to its original state as a plain wall made of square mirror tiles. In the reflection of the far wall, Eli saw something sparkly descending from the ceiling. Looking up, Eli saw an old-time-looking shiny red key floating down from the ceiling. When the key reached Eli, he grasped the key. The key was heavy, like it was made out of iron but looked like it was made out of bright red glass. When Eli closed his hand on the key, the mirror tiles on the floor to Eli's left lit up, forming a path that led to one of four doors that Eli noticed for the first time lined the wall of the movie-theatre room.

These doors were different colors and each had different features. The door Eli was walking toward was red, like the key, made from a thick iron material that reminded Eli of a large cauldron, and had flames etched into it. There was also a green door made of wood with vines, a black door made of what looked like some sort of animal skin with feathers, and a fourth door that was hard to see because it looked like a large mirror and blended in with the wall. None of these doors had any handles or knobs, only a large golden keyhole located in the center of each door.

Cautiously, Eli walked down the lit path of tiles to the red door with the flames. As Eli walked, he noticed his reflection in the mirror tiles walked ahead of him and stood by the door. It was his flesh again. Not even looking at his flesh, Eli walked up and placed the key in the door's lock.

"You really are going in that room." Eli's flesh laughed in a tone of disbelief. "I can't believe it. I can't believe that you would be so stupid to ignore the obvious fact that what awaits you in this room has something to do with the seeds in the film that burst into flames and died! I have only one thing to say to you; I will enjoy watching you burn!"

Eli's flesh disappeared as his mocking laughter echoed through the room and down the hall. Determined, Eli turned the key and heard the lock in the door click. Suddenly the door burst into flames. Eli jumped back, startled. The flames continued but Eli did not feel any heat from the flames nor did the fire from the door singe any of his clothing. Eli watched and realized the flames were holographic. The flames subsided and the door cracked open. Taking a few deep breaths to calm his nerves, Eli reassured himself with the words from the Man in the film.

"I love you, my child, and am eager to welcome you when you gain the victory." Feeling resolved, Eli pushed open the door and entered the room of fire.

chapter 18
the room of fire

Eli crossed over the threshold and was instantly overwhelmed by the most oppressive heat he had ever experienced. Eli's senses were momentarily rendered useless. Stumbling forward a few steps, Eli fell to his knees and covered his face. Falling down did not help Eli at all because the ground was so hot that it felt like Eli was kneeling on a hot stove. Eli stood up and turned, thinking that he would walk back out the door for a moment, when he noticed the door was already closed. Not wanting to risk looking like he was giving up, Eli turned to face the room and tried to acclimate to this new challenge.

The room was a large cavern that looked like the inside of a very active and deadly volcano. The ground and walls consisted of a shiny black stone and the ceiling of the room was obscured by what appeared to be a hazardous cloud formed from all the vapors rising out of the rocks and lava.

On the far end of the room was a climbing wall and on top of that climbing wall was a shiny green key resting on a golden podium. In between Eli and the green key were three sections of rock separated by two large rivers of lava. The first section, which began at Eli's feet, was what looked like a black slip-n-slide of death. It was a steep decline of dangerously smooth black rock full of random razor sharp shards. The death slide ended into the first river of lava that ran left to right in the room. Above the lava river were several floating black stones. These stones ascended upward to the other bank of the lava river that was significantly higher than the bank nearest Eli. On the other side of that river was a long plain followed by another river with a beautiful white bridge allowing access to the final section of rock on which the climbing wall with the key stood.

Already feeling the oppressive heat drain his strength and cloud his mind, Eli began to walk down the steep smooth decline toward the river of lava. Eli placed his right foot onto the steep path slowly and when he felt he had sufficient grip he then brought his left foot down. Standing in what Eli felt was a surfer's stance on the slope, he began to slide down the path with his lead foot catching on the bumps of rocks for grip. Eli's speed started to increase and instinctively, Eli reached down and grabbed hold of a larger stone on the border of the path. The stone, however, was razor sharp and extremely hot. In a moment Eli jerked back his hand that was now blistered and bleeding. This sudden movement threw Eli off balance. Before Eli could regain his balance, he fell backwards on his back and was sliding down the steep slope heading into the river of lava like he was on a water slide going toward the pool.

All the small jagged rocks on the path were now cutting and slicing Eli's back and legs as he cascaded down toward the lava. Eli tried to slow himself down with his hands, but only managed to acquire more cuts and burns.

Eli could see the end of the path approaching rapidly and knew he had to do something soon or else he would be swimming in the river of lava. Looking around wildly, Eli saw his only chance for survival: a large boulder bordering the left side of the path. This boulder looked tall enough to stop Eli's body and it looked blunt enough to not slice him in half. The boulder was only about ten feet away now and the river bank was only another five to ten feet after that. Summoning all of his strength, Eli threw his right hand down on the path and at the same time kicked with his right leg and flipped himself off the side of the path, crashing into the boulder.

Yelping out in pain, Eli successfully stopped his descent into the river of lava, but he had also slammed his right rib cage into the scalding hot boulder. As carefully as he could, Eli picked himself off the ground and tried to stand. The pain surging throughout his body told him that he had just lived through a trip down the slip-n-slide of death by possibly cracking a few ribs, but at least he had survived. Eli could feel the trickles of blood flow down his back and legs from the numerous cuts he suffered as he slid, but all in all, Eli was still alive and that was something to be thankful for.

Eli planted his right foot on the rock and then slowly made his way down to the river bank. When Eli reached the bank a glowing piece of parchment appeared floating in front of him.

The parchment read:

The River of Resolve

Crossing this river will not be easy;

Don't look down or you might get queasy.

Underneath each rock on every side,

A deadly liquid if you touch you die.

To find success you better heed;

You must move forward with accurate speed.

Soon you will find the rock you're on,

Will vanish quickly and be gone.

If there is any doubt return to your ways earthly,

"For the person who looks back is not worthy."

Eli looked up from the parchment at the stones hovering in the air. There were nine stones in all and all the stones were in the shape of rectangles about the size of Eli's parent's living room rug. The stones bridged the two banks of the river with increasing distance between them and also increased in height as they approached the other bank of the river.

Eli took a moment to examine the challenge while one line from the parchment rattled around in his head.

"Soon you will find the rock you're on will vanish quickly and be gone."

Eli took a few moments to plan his journey across the rocks above the river before stepping up to the edge of the bank. Feeling the heat from the river of lava rush over him gave Eli an adrenaline rush. Stepping back a few feet, Eli took a running start and leapt onto the first stone with a yell of determination. Landing on his feet, Eli was surprised at how stable and solid the floating rock felt under him. A loud ticking noise that reminded Eli of his grandfather's large pendulum clock erupted throughout the room. The ticks were long and slow, but as Eli prepared to make the next leap, he noticed the ticks increasing in speed.

Heeding the parchment's warning to move quickly, Eli made the leap to the second stone positioned a little farther from the first stone with a minor incline. Again, Eli landed squarely on the stone without incident. The ticks continued to increase. When they were sounding in rapid sequence Eli heard a loud splash. Turning around Eli noticed the first stone fell from its place and crashed into the lava. Once again the ticking began, only this time it started at a faster pace than before.

So that is how it works, thought Eli. *I had better hurry. I will need to save some time to prepare for the longer jumps at the end.*

The next several stones continued to spread further from each other and the incline continued to increase, but Eli was sure that he could jump them without taking too much time. As the ticking continued to increase, Eli jumped across the next several stones. When Eli reached the last stone which he considered an easier leap, the second stone crashed into the lava. The ticking restarted and as Eli predicted was faster than before. Eli had only three more stones to jump, and had four stones still in the air behind him. Taking his time Eli regrouped and observed his next leap. It would be about five feet across and two feet up. Eli walked to the back of the stone he stood on and was about to run forward when he heard a much louder than anticipated splash. Turning and gasping in horror, Eli saw that this time two stones crashed into the lava leaving only two behind him. Further, the ticking sound began at a pace that Eli knew did not allow much time before the next set of stones fell. Taking deep breaths to focus, Eli looked forward, ran, and made the leap to the next stone.

"Two more stones and then the jump to the bank," said Eli, catching his breath.

Before he could gather his breath, another loud crash rang through the room as two more stones fell into the lava. The ticking again began at a high rate and Eli realized the stone he was standing on would be in the next group to fall. The terror of being melted in lava pushed Eli to hurry in his preparations to jump. Eli ran to the end of the stone and just as his foot left the stone, the stone fell into the lava. Yelling out of surprise Eli landed and rolled on the next stone. Not taking any time to look, Eli stood up, ran as fast as he could and leaped into the air. This time, only the top half of his body made it to the next stone and his legs hung over the edge. Pulling himself up, Eli observed the final leap to the bank. It was farther than he would have liked, and it was still about two feet higher than the stone on which he now stood. Motivated by the rapid sound of the ticking, knowing that it was now or never, Eli ran toward the end of the stone ready to leap.

Then it happened. The ticking ended and the stone began its descent into the lava. Eli took one more step and flung himself toward the bank of the river. Things seemed to slow down as Eli saw the bank of the river approach and realized he would not make it all the way. Eli's body slammed into the bank with only his arms, head, and shoulders landing on the bank. Eli's body, from his chest to his feet dangled over the edge of the river's bank. Eli's ribs shouted in pain as they were once again slammed against the black stone. His arms, which were already bloody and bruised, burned so bad that Eli considered letting go.

"No, I can do this!" yelled Eli as he slowly pulled himself up.

Fortunately, the shoes he received at the castle had great grip and Eli was able to plant his feet and push himself onto the rock. Eli rolled over on his back and wanted to lie there in victory but the oppressive heat from the stone felt like it was cooking his body. Eli quickly rolled over and stood to his feet. The intense heat made his eyes burn and his throat hurt. Eli was not sure how it was possible, but it felt as if the room's temperature had increased as he entered into this new section of rock. As before, when Eli was able to stand on the bank of the river, a glowing parchment appeared in front of him.

The parchment read:

The Searing Stone

There is no lava in this task to bemoan,

Just cross a plain of smooth black stone.

The task is so simple you need not cheat,

To pass this test, simply beat the heat.

As you pass through this task you will soon find

A scorching test of heart, will, and mind.

The task is not easy; it will cause you to stumble.

The key to success is learn to be humble.

Success comes with the admonition,

"If any will come after Me,

they will suffer affliction."

Eli looked up from the parchment to the plain of flat black stone. It did not look dangerous nor did it look as if the heat on the plain could be any more intense than the heat Eli was currently feeling. At the end of the plain was a large bridge that crossed the second river of lava stream and connected to the last section on which the climbing wall resided. Anticipating a nasty twist in this task, Eli began his journey across the plain.

Eli took off running across the plain knowing that the sooner he reached the other side the sooner whatever twist he was sure was going to happen would be over. Several steps into his run, a large dome appeared on the plain forming a transparent bubble. Inside the dome, the heat's intensity more than doubled to the point in which the very air seemed to be burning and blistering Eli's skin. Eli tried to continue running but the heat was wreaking havoc on his senses. It was hard to see and breathe as the heat burned his eyes, skin, and lungs. The heat was so intense it distorted Eli's sight and everything looked like it was waving in the air. Eli found that he had to slow down in order to ensure he was heading in the right direction. As he continued through the dome he felt the heat sapping his strength. Before he knew it, his run through the dome had slowed to an excruciatingly slow walk. The heat grew so intense that it felt as if a heavy weight was squashing him toward the ground. Every step forced Eli to use an incredible amount of energy. After several steps, Eli looked up and realized he was not more than halfway across the plain. Extreme dizziness overwhelmed Eli and he quickly became discombobulated. Eli fell forward to the ground. The rocks burned his skin giving Eli enough strength to push his body up but he could not stand up. Eli knelt on his knees ready to give up when a cool breeze brushed across Eli's face. Shocked and momentarily refreshed, Eli opened his eyes. As he did so, he realized his eyes were not burning, nor were his lungs hurting from the intense heat of the room. Rather, it seemed as if Eli found a cool jet stream surging through the dome. As Eli knelt there he also realized that even the rocks underneath him that scorched his skin moments ago seemed cool to the touch. Confused, but grateful, Eli stood back up to continue but as soon as he got off his knees the scorching heat returned and warred against his senses. Eli immediately dropped back to his knees and once again experienced the cool stream of air and felt the cool stone under his knees.

That's it! thought Eli. *The key to success is learn to be humble.*

Eli's mind went back to a time when he walked in on his grandfather praying on his knees. When Eli asked why he knelt, his grandfather told him it helped him be humble before the Lord. By kneeling, it showed his inferiority before God and declared his dependence on Him.

Eli began to walk on his knees through the dome. As he did so, the air remained cool and so did the rocks; however, the rocks cut and bruised his knees.

I get it, thought Eli. *The King will protect and refresh those who humble themselves before Him, but there is still a price to be paid for discipleship.*

Eli continued his painful yet cool trek through the scorching stone plane until he approached the large bridge. Just as suddenly as it appeared, the scorching dome barrier disappeared. Eli stood up, and the pain from his knees joined with the other wounds and bruises that now surged through his body as the room's heat renewed its attack.

Two down, one more to go! thought Eli excitedly.

Eli looked at the bridge that would take him to the base of the climbing wall on top of which his goal rested. The bridge was a bright white metal with gold hand rails. The bridge seemed out of place in Eli's mind because it reminded him of the bridge at the park in his home town. This quaint arch bridge reminded Eli of peace, happiness and beauty, all of which were a far cry from his present situation. Eli crossed the bridge focused on the last task set before him. At the end of the bridge, another parchment appeared.

The Scorching Wall

One more riddle, one more rhyme,

One Scorching wall, only one time.

What you see is what you get;

The key at the top your next door will fit.

Be so careful to hold and not tumble;

Not only is it hot, this wall will rumble.

The test of fire entering this room you began,

Will all disappear when the key you have in hand.

Eli surveyed his last task. The wall was as tall as a three-story building and was completely surrounded by a mote of lava save for a skinny walkway leading from the bridge to the wall. The mountain itself was solid black stone with jagged rocks protruding out all around. Eli knew that he would have to climb up the mound using the rocks as hand grips and steps. Eli slowly approached the mountain. As he approached he could feel the heat radiating off the mountain hitting him like a wall. The heat was not as intense as the heat in the dome, but in the dome, Eli did not have to grab hold of the stone. Eli crossed the skinny walkway and could feel the lava under him and all around him. The heat of the lava once again caused all of Eli's wounds to cry out in pain as if the heat and his pain were somehow connected. Placing his hand on the wall, Eli touched the stone. Just as Eli thought, the stone was extremely hot and burned his hand.

The knowledge of the coming pain this task would require froze Eli in position for several moments. Eli's body was in a constant state of pain. The cuts and bruises from his initial slide down the slope continued to sting and ache. Eli's ribs and knees were swollen and sore, and his eyes and lungs burned from the heat of the air. Now, to finish this task, Eli would have to climb up a mountain of burning hot stone.

Motivating himself for the final task, Eli kept repeating, "'...will all disappear when the key you have in hand.' Don't know what that means but I like the sound of it."

Gritting his teeth, Eli began his painful climb. The rocks were large enough to get good grips on without slipping or sliding. The location of the rocks also made the climb easy, from a tactical standpoint. The problem was the rocks felt like hot irons and burned every part of Eli's body that made contact with them. Eli had not gone but about ten feet up when he heard a loud deep rumble in the cavern and suddenly the wall began to rumble. Eli grabbed the mountain with both hands and pulled himself close to the stone. The rumbling, however, shook his whole body and caused his face to get smashed up against the stone. Eli screamed and instinctively let go. Falling, Eli tried to get his feet underneath him to land but could not get them square before he hit. Eli felt and heard a loud pop in his left ankle and a surge of pain shot through his body. Eli rolled on the burning ground holding his ankle writhing in pain. The pain in his ankle was so intense that Eli forgot about the narrowness of the path and rolled off the side of the walkway, plummeting to the lava. Letting go of his ankle, Eli just barely had time to grab hold of the narrow walkway and prevent his fall into the lava river. Calling out in pain, Eli was able to lift himself back on the walkway and lie on his back clutching his ankle. The skin on his back burned but the pain in his ankle trumped everything. Already, his ankle began to swell and Eli knew that it was broken or fractured.

As the shock of the injury calmed down, Eli struggled to his feet and hopped back to the wall.

"That was so dumb!" shouted Eli. "The parchment said the mountain would rumble. I should have expected it."

Eli carefully tested his ankle by attempting to place weight on it. Eli knew his ankle was hurt, but he also knew he could alleviate the amount he used his left leg by using his hands and right leg to do most of the climbing.

Slowly and surely, Eli once again began his climb up the mountain. Though his progress was slow and extremely painful, he moved in a way that would help him cope with the burning of the stone and the occasional rumbling of the mountain. The higher up Eli climbed the less hot the mountain became. Though it was still hot, the higher stone was farther from the lava and felt welcome against his stinging skin. On the flip side, the higher up Eli climbed the stronger and more violent the rumbling. As Eli approached the top of the mountain the rumbling caused the top to actually sway back and forth as stone crumbled down the mountain. Finally, Eli reached the top and pulled himself onto the little area of flat stone.

Standing to his feet, or foot as it were since Eli kept his left foot elevated off the ground, Eli smiled with a sense of victory. There in front of him, just a little out of arms reach was the golden podium with the shiny green key. Eli took a hop toward the podium. Just as Eli landed the mountain rumbled again catching Eli off guard. To steady himself his body automatically plunged his left foot down for balance. As his foot slammed into the stone a jolt of blinding pain erupted from his ankle causing Eli to tumble forward into the podium. Eli looked up in slow motion as the key flew off the podium into the air. Eli's eyes widened as he watched the key go over the side of the mountain toward the river of lava beneath. Eli was afraid that if the key fell into the lava he would fail his mission and threw himself off the mountain toward the key. As they plummeted toward the lava all Eli could focus on was the key. Eli quickly caught up with the key. Seeing the river of lava, and subsequently his own death, racing toward him, Eli reached out his hand and desperately wrapped his fingers around the key. Eli then closed his eyes and braced himself for what would be his last moments in life before his body splashed into the lava.

Sure enough, Eli felt his body splash into a stingy liquid. The liquid shocked Eli's body, but to Eli's surprise, the liquid was not melting him; it was refreshing him. Eli opened his eyes to see that he had fallen into a crystal clear stream of water. Eli swam to the surface and looked around at the room of fire.

Everything had changed. The tortuous room full of burning stone, lava, and poisonous fumes now resembled the courtyard of Eden! The streams of glowing lava were now streams of crystal clear water. All the scorching black stone was now thick luscious grass. The barren plain was now covered in trees and the lifeless room of death was buzzing with life. Animals of all kinds walked throughout the room in perfect harmony. The air that was so hot and abusive was pleasant and full of the most fragrant aromas. The only thing that did not change was the beautiful white bridge which now looked as if it fit its surroundings.

Pulling himself out of the water, Eli could not resist the urge to roll around in the thick cool grass. Lying in the grass, Eli realized all the pain in his body was gone. All the cuts, bruises, burns, and broken bones suffered in this room were totally healed. Even Eli's clothes were mended as if they were brand new.

"You see, my child," echoed the Man's voice from the film into Eli's mind. "One day I will make all things new. Though this world will rage against you with all of its hate and bitterness attempting to burn away your resolve to live for me, when your task is finished, there will be peace and comfort. This world is suffering the consequences of sin, but one day, the very fire it will try to destroy you with will be the fire that consumes it. One day I will make a new heaven and a new earth free from the curse of sin. On that day, you will see the great difference between temporary suffering and eternal rejoicing."

His heart burning inside of him from the voice of the Man, Eli lay in the grass as a large shadow covered his face. Looking up, Eli saw a male lion, just like the one he saw in the courtyard of Eden approach him and lie next to him. The lion, which was obviously seeking attention from Eli, nearly crushed Eli as he rolled over trying to get his head into Eli's hands.

The green key in one hand, Eli laughed and rolled on his side to scratch the gigantic cat behind his ears. As he did so, the lion purred and several lion cubs ran over to join in on the fun. Before long, Eli had a large group of lions, lion cubs, and other large cats all vying for his affection. Witnessing a world full of creatures without the taint of sin overwhelmed Eli with the desire to be a part of the new heaven and new earth.

Knowing that his task was not over, Eli stood up, said goodbye to the animals, and walked toward the beginning of the room. As he walked, Eli continued to pet the different animals in his path and was awed by the perfect harmony the absence of sin brought to all creatures. Looking over the river bank, Eli saw a beautiful crystal river where the lava river was earlier. Knowing the only appropriate action for him to take was a flying cannon ball, Eli threw himself off the cliff and splashed into the crystal clear water of the river.

Eli swam across the river and made his way back up the slope toward the door. The slope which was now covered with grass and vegetation was far easier to ascend than it was to descend. The material of Eli's new clothes must have been water resistant because by the time Eli made it up the slope, he was completely dry. Eli stopped in front of the door he entered what seemed like an eternity ago. Fighting the desire to remain in the room longer and knowing that he had a mission to complete, Eli took one last deep breath of the cool refreshing air and exited the room.

chapter 19
the room of thorns

Eli stepped back into the movie-theatre-like room and closed the door behind him. When the door closed, it started glowing with a bright red light. The light's brightness increased until the door was no longer visible. In a moment the light was gone, and so was the door. Where the door had been in the wall, there was only glass tile.

Eli looked at his reflection and saw that he still had the burns, cuts, bruises, and blood. For a moment, Eli panicked, until he realized the reflection he was looking at was his flesh.

"Wow!" said Eli. "You must have really enjoyed watching me burn in that room. It looks like you enjoyed it so much that you decided to go through it personally."

"Look who thinks he is a comedian," quipped Eli's flesh, obviously in pain. "You think that just because you survived the first room by the very skin of your teeth that you are going to be victorious? Don't make me laugh. Do you not realize how close to death you were in that room? I counted less than two seconds. There were less than two seconds between you grabbing that key and falling in the river that would have been lava!"

"We have covered all of this before. I am not going to quit. Coming close to dying in that room only showed me that I have what it takes to succeed for my King. All you have done by appearing again is to show me that I am winning; you are suffering defeat and soon you will die."

"I will never die!" yelled Eli's flesh. "I know what awaits you in these rooms. I know how strong your desires are. I know how strong the Enemy is, and I know a secret that you don't know. I can't wait to watch you suffer. Just remember when you find yourself dying in these rooms; I might be burned, but I'm still alive. I will dance on your tomb and I will take all that I have and serve my master whom you call Enemy once you are gone. Farewell, Eli. I hope you choke on your desires!"

The reflection of Eli's flesh returned to a normal reflection of Eli. A new path of lit tiles started at Eli's feet and led to the green door that looked like it was made out of wood. Understanding now that the parable of the sower and the tasks before him were intimately connected, Eli had an idea of what awaited him inside this next room.

Eli approached the door and placed the green key into the key hole, and turned the key as a new hologram erupted on the door. Prepared for the hologram, Eli did not jump back but rather took a few steps back to observe the door. Knowing now that the hologram was an indication of what was inside the door, Eli chose to take a little more time to meditate upon the warning. Springing from the door were beautiful green vines. These vines sprouted gorgeous flowers of all colors as they spiraled upward and climbed the wall of the room. As the vines thickened into maturity, Eli noticed that large sharp thorns grew underneath the beautiful petals of the flowers.

"Thorns," said Eli. "Surely they cannot be as painful as fire!"

The memory of the burns and injuries suffered in the room of fire prompted Eli to re-examine his body and make sure they had all been healed. Satisfied that he was his pre-cooked self again, Eli opened the door and entered the room of thorns.

Eli stepped through the door with his eyes closed. He wanted to take his time and slowly see the task in front of him as he was ready. When Eli opened his eyes, he was startled and confused. The room Eli was looking at was nothing more than white, empty space. Eli could see no walls, no floor, no ceiling, and no colors of any sort. The only thing in the room was a golden podium with a black shiny key resting on top of it at the far end of the room. The podium caught Eli's attention because of the contrast between the pure white nothingness and also because attached to the podium was a thick rope that lay on the ground toward Eli that stretched about ten feet from the podium. Something about that rope made Eli pause.

Why would there be a rope? thought Eli as he shook his head to rid all the awful fears that began forming in his mind. "It doesn't matter! I am going to get that key and become a defender and I am going to do it no matter what may come."

Before Eli could take a step forward, a blinding light flashed out of the nothingness above, temporarily blinding Eli, and scanned his body. Eli rubbed his burning eyes and tried to blink the bright spots out of his vision. When Eli's vision cleared, the room had changed. No longer was the room one large white space of nothingness; it was now a large meadow filled with beautiful flowers. The meadow was divided into three equal sections that covered the entire room.

The first section of the room was covered in beautiful red roses, the second section of the room was covered in golden daisies, and the third section of the room was covered in beautiful flowers with royal blue and deep purple coloring. Though Eli had never really been a fan of flowers, something about this room and these flowers made Eli feel happy.

This is incredible! thought Eli. *This room is nothing like what I thought it was going to be. This room looks more like paradise than a challenge.*

At that moment, Eli remembered what the Man had said in the film about the enemies he would face as well as his flesh's rant against him moments ago.

"The Man said I would have to face the world, my own desires, the Enemy, and my flesh. I battled the world in the fire room. I'm pretty sure I would recognize the room with the Enemy, and I don't see my flesh in here anywhere; this must be the room where I face my own desires. That's why my flesh said he hoped I would choke on my desires."

Eli recalled the seeds that had been chocked by thorns, as well as the hologram of the beautiful flowers hiding nasty thorns, and suddenly this pleasant room of flowers did not seem so inviting. Eli looked back at the rope tied to the podium as a sense of fear as to the purpose of the rope's existence washed over him.

"Why would you be afraid in a room like this?" called out a girl's voice.

"Yes," added a man's voice. "This is not a room of fear; this is a room of blessings. We are not here to hurt you; we are here to help you enjoy life."

Eli scanned the room for the source of the voices as three individuals were suddenly standing in the room. A beautiful teenage girl about Eli's age wearing a beautiful dress appeared in the roses. Behind her, in the section of golden daisies appeared a middle-aged man, dressed as a butler with a skinny mustache and balding head. In the final section of the room with the royal blue and purple flowers stood a man dressed as a king in beautiful robes wearing a large golden crown.

"I don't understand," said Eli as he tried to deal with the shock of the sudden appearance of other people. "Who are you and what are you doing here?"

The girl giggled and spoke first. "My name is Iris, and my job is to help you experience the joy of love."

Eli's face flushed with color and he could feel his palms start to sweat as the beautiful girl looked at him like she was in love with him.

"My name," began the butler in an elegant and smooth voice, "is Crave, and I am here to serve you and to bring you anything your heart desires."

"And my name," spoke the man dressed as a king whose voice Eli had heard earlier, "is Pol, and I am here to help you achieve all that you want to achieve in life."

"But what about the battle or challenge that I would have to face to retrieve that key and proceed to the next room?" asked Eli.

"Battle? Oh no!" said Iris in a compassionate tone. "You have already fought a battle in that terrible room of fire. Now that you are victorious, we thought you could use a room to rest, relax, and enjoy life for a little bit."

"Thank you," replied Eli, "but I think I am just going to get that key and move on."

"Are you kidding me?" said Pol. "How do you ever expect to be a defender and to lead other people if you don't allow yourself time to recuperate? Even the greatest leaders understand the need to enjoy life! How are you going to be able to lead others to health and happiness if you are not readily enjoying them personally?"

Before Eli could respond, Iris walked up to him, kissed him on the cheek and handed him a rose.

"Here, just take a moment to smell this rose and then tell me that you don't have the time to take just a few minutes and enjoy this great room of blessing before you get your key and continue your difficult and thankless journey."

Disarmed by the kiss, Eli took the rose from Iris and sniffed it. A greenish cloud of scent emanated from the rose filling Eli's nostrils and mouth. Immediately Eli was filled with a warm feeling and a desire to stay in the room and enjoy all there was to enjoy before moving on.

"You know what?" said Eli with a goofy grin on his face. "I think I will stay here for a little while."

"Wonderful choice!" said Crave. "Now that you are staying with us, what would you like for me to get you?"

"Are you telling me that I can ask for anything?" asked Eli.

"Whatever you desire," responded Crave with a greedy smile on his face.

Turning toward Pol, Eli asked, "I don't know, Pol. What do you think I should ask for?"

"Well, I can't speak for everyone," said Pol. "But if I was you and I had a beautiful girl wanting to spend time with me, I would ask for a nice place I could take her for dinner and some amazingly good food."

"That's a great idea!" said Eli as he saw Iris look at him and smile. "Crave, I would love a nice dinner table, some chairs, and some food. I have a lovely young lady who deserves the best."

"Brilliantly said!" replied Crave.

Crave snapped his fingers and a dinner table appeared in the middle of the patch of roses complete with candles and Eli's favorite food: pizza. Crave then snapped his fingers again and two chairs appeared next to the table.

"Hold on right there," interrupted Pol. "Those chairs are for normal people, not esteemed guests. I do believe Master Eli deserves a chair fit for a king."

"Yes," agreed Iris. "I want my love to experience everything he desires without any discomfort at all."

"As you wish," said Crave as he snapped his fingers and replaced Eli's original chair with a large, luscious throne-like chair. This chair had a solid gold frame and four beautifully carved wooden legs. The frame of the chair was covered with ornate carvings that depicted Eli as a king and a ruler. The cushion and back cushion of the chair were made out of the softest royal blue material Eli had ever felt.

"That is the most amazing chair I have ever seen!" said Eli as he ran his finger from the cushion to the scenes of him as a ruler. "Are these scenes real? I mean, is this what I am going to be in life or did you just make them up?"

Pol walked up beside Eli. "Oh no, we did not make these up. These scenes are what you can have in life. These scenes are what we desire you to have in life and the longer you stick with us, the more of these scenes you will experience. Please, sire, have a seat."

"Oh no, I can't sit down yet," said Eli in a serious manner.

For a brief moment, Eli thought he saw Pol's face flare with rage and his eyes burn with a red light before Pol smiled at Eli and asked, "Why not?"

"Because," said Eli, trying to convince himself what he saw was only in his mind, "I have not allowed my date to sit first."

"Oh, of course," said Crave as he walked around the table and pulled the chair out for Iris.

"Thank you, sir," said Iris to Crave before turning her gaze over to Eli. "And thank you for being a gentleman. I am seated, now, would my love also sit down so we can enjoy this incredible looking pizza?"

Eli sat down and as he did he felt his body sink into the cushions as if the cushions were wrapping themselves around his body. Crave and Pol walked up beside Eli on both sides of the throne-like chair.

"Let us make you more comfortable," said Pol as he motioned to Crave.

Crave examined Eli for a moment and then placed a napkin on his lap and a napkin around his neck.

"There, that ought to make it where we do not get pizza all over your clothes. Speaking of your clothes," continued Crave, "they need to be updated as soon as possible."

"And they will be," said Pol, "just as soon as Master Eli finishes his dinner."

Eli looked down at the napkins and when he looked up, Iris was standing right in front of him with a delicious looking piece of meat-lover's pizza in her hand.

"Here, Eli, I want you to take the first bite," Iris said as she wrapped her legs around his legs.

Completely mesmerized by the great blessings of this room, Eli closed his eyes, opened his mouth, and took a bite as he realized Iris' legs were literally wrapping around his.

Instead of tasting the warm gooey cheese and flavorful meat that Eli was anticipating, Eli experienced incredible pain in his mouth and tasted blood. Yelling out, Eli spit the pizza out, only it was not pizza it was chewed up thorns!

Eli went to grab his throat as he began choking on his blood, but found he could not lift his arms off of the chair.

When Eli looked down at his arms, fear engulfed him and he realized that he had allowed himself to be fooled.

Growing out from underneath the beautiful covering of roses were the nasty thorn vines Eli saw in the hologram. These vines had wrapped themselves up Eli's legs and around his arms, tying him to the chair. The more Eli struggled, the more the thorns cut into his body causing agonizing pain. As for Iris, Crave, and Pol, they were standing off to the side of Eli laughing as they watched him squirm.

"What's the matter Eli?" called out Iris. "Don't like the taste of my cooking? Don't worry, you won't be alive long enough to enjoy dessert!"

Just then large thorn vines wrapped around the table and broke the table in half. The pieces of the table were then dragged back through the patch of roses and sucked into a hole. Once inside the hole, Eli heard what sounded like a buzz saw and watched as sawdust and small splinters of wood sprayed out of the hole. With the table gone, the large vines shot out of the hole and were coming for Eli. Struggling with all his might, Eli was able to break the vines holding his right arm to the chair and shake off the thorns that were stuck in his arm. Working feverishly on the vines holding his left arm down, Eli just freed his other arm when the large vines reached the chair and wrapped themselves around the base of the chair.

The vines squeezed the chair, breaking off the thick wooden legs, and began dragging the chair towards the hole. When the vines pulled the chair, the chair tipped over and Eli was able to grab hold of one of the chair's broken legs. Using the broken leg as a knife, Eli first pierced the vines that were dragging him toward the hole and then, when they released the chair, used the leg to cut his legs free. Free from the vines and the chair, Eli turned toward the podium with the key and took off running.

"No!" shouted Iris. "You will not escape me!"

Iris raised her hands and a wall of nasty thorn vines began rising out of the ground on the border of the section of roses and the section of daisies. Eli made it to the border just as the wall of thorns was about chest high. Eli jumped over the wall with his upper body but his lower body crashed through the thorns in the wall.

Eli tumbled on the ground in the golden daisies as Iris let out a rage filled scream. Eli did not care about Iris at this point because of the pain shooting through his legs. Examining his legs, Eli saw that the wall of thorns left several long and deep cuts on his legs to go with the minor cuts from the thorn vines that bound him to the chair. Every movement set Eli's legs ablaze with intense pain, but Eli knew he did not have the luxury of lying on the ground. The room of thorns had shown its true nature and Eli knew his life was in danger.

Standing up as fast as he could, Eli turned to see the podium with the key but discovered his view was completely barred by a solid wall of giant thorn vines. Standing in front of the wall was Crave, looking smug and uninterested.

"Good for you," said Crave. "Not every defender has the ability to overcome the lust of the eyes. Personally, I feel that a human's attachment to other humans and their lust for beauty and pleasure to be pointless and uninteresting. The lust of the eyes is too unstable for me. You see, I, the lust of your flesh, like to work with solids. Tell me, Eli, what is something you want more than anything else?"

Eli stood there in shock as he listened to Crave, and even though he refused to speak any words, a picture of the electric guitar that he had been wanting since his friend got one popped into his mind.

"Oh, very nice," said Crave as he snapped his fingers.

Instantly Eli heard the sound of something falling and before he could look up, the electric guitar crashed onto his back sending Eli rolling to the ground.

"I guess that is why they call it 'Rock and Roll,'" said Crave as he laughed to himself. "But seriously, what about your dream Blue-Ray collection?"

Eli tried not to think about anything but soon he heard the sound of falling objects and instead of standing still, Eli jumped to his feet and ran to his right as fast as he could with his hurt legs as Blue-Ray disks, nearly a hundred of them, flew at Eli like ninja-stars. Most of the disks missed Eli but several sliced Eli's back, arms, and legs.

"This is fun!" said Crave. "Now that you are warmed up, let's move on to the important things in life. Tell me, Master Eli, what car would you be willing to give up everything for?"

Eli felt nauseous, as if he were going to throw up as the 1969 Camaro Eli had a poster of in his room popped into his mind.

"Ah yes," said Crave. "A very nice choice!"

Crave snapped his fingers and Eli saw a shadow surround him and heard the sound of something falling. Moving as fast as his damaged legs could, Eli jumped and rolled out from under the shadow just in time to see the Camaro he pictured in his mind crash to the ground where he was standing.

"Bravo!" said Crave. "I cannot tell you how many defenders spend their lives chasing after nice vehicles. But I grow weary of this game. I so desire to see you eliminated. Tell me, Mr. Storm, what do you picture when you picture your dream house?"

Eli knew what his mind would see, Eli knew that there was nothing he could do to stop it, and Eli knew that if Crave were to bring that house down in this section that it would crush Eli to death. There was only one way Eli could figure he would survive what he knew was coming and that was to plow through the wall of thorns.

Crave's laughter interrupted Eli's thoughts and told him that his mind did indeed send Crave the picture of the mansion. As a shadow formed above Eli that covered the entire section of flowers, Eli ran for the wall.

"You will never make it," yelled out Crave. "You will be crushed by the lust of your flesh!"

The noise of something gigantic falling filled Eli's ears. Just a few feet from the wall of thorns, Eli covered his face with his arms and dove through the wall. Eli felt the wall of thorns break apart and he felt something massive scrape down the bottom of his shoe followed by a ground-shaking crash behind him. This time, it was Crave's rage-filled screams that filled the room but once again, Eli could not care less about the screams of others because he was doing his best to hold back his own screams.

Eli rolled to a sitting position on the royal blue and purple flowers, shaking from pain as he examined his body. Three large thorns were sticking out of him. One thorn was sticking through his right foot, one thorn was sticking out of his left thigh, and Eli had one thorn sticking out of his chest. Slowly, with shaking hands, Eli pulled the thorns out of his foot and thigh. Then, after assessing the situation, Eli slowly and painfully took the thorn out of his chest. Blood poured from the wounds. Eli began coughing and tasted blood again, but not the blood from his mouth—blood from his lungs. Knowing his time to get that key was short, Eli stood to his feet not knowing what to expect.

"Tisk, tisk, tisk. Look at you," said Pol. "I must say, I am impressed. However, you will never achieve your greatest ambitions looking like that."

Barely able to stand, Eli looked at Pol. "What are you talking about? Who are you?"

"You don't know by now?" began Pol. "Think about it. You met the lust of the eyes in Iris; you met the lust of your flesh in Crave; there is only one more powerful desire in life and that is the pride of life. It is true I did not get a witty name like Iris or Crave, but when you are the king, you don't need witty names."

"So you're the king?" Eli laughed. "What makes you so special?" asked Eli as he tried his best to look unimpressed.

"Insolent boy!" roared Pol. "I am no mere desire. I am the *original* desire! Birthed by the Enemy himself in the very presence of perfection, it was I, the pride of life, who told the Enemy that he ought to be King. It is I who put the ambition in the mind of the Enemy to rise up and to lead one third of the King's ministers against the King in battle. Do you understand now? The Enemy himself was devoured by me. What makes you think that a mere human boy could ever withstand my power?"

Not wanting to communicate how shocked he was by what Pol just revealed, Eli responded just as unimpressed as before. "Well then, your *majesty*, how do you intend on killing me? Are you going to trick me like Iris, crush me like Crave, or are you just going to make my head swell with pride so much that it explodes?"

"Very witty." Pol chuckled. "But no, ambitions do not lead you into destruction through temptation or crush you with the weight of material things. Ambitions devour you whole!"

Pol laughed insanely as he sank into the ground. Eli looked in front of him and saw that there was no wall of thorns or anything else between him and the golden podium with the key. Not waiting for something terrible to appear, Eli hobbled over toward the podium as fast as he could. The wounds in his foot, thigh, and chest made Eli's trek slow and painful but soon Eli made it to the edge of the rope unhindered. Eli bent down and picked up the rope when the ground began to rumble.

Turning around Eli saw a giant, man-eating plant spring up from the ground in the middle of the royal blue and purple flower section. The plant sprung out of the ground at least twenty to thirty feet into the air, with the entire upper half of the plant one gigantic mouthful of razor sharp teeth dripping with saliva. At the base of the plant were several large thorn vines that the plant moved like arms.

"Selfish ambition," roared Pol's voice gurgling out of the giant plant's mouth, "has devoured so many potential defenders; and now, Eli Storm, it will devour you."

The plant's vines shot toward Eli attempting to grab his ankles. Eli evaded the first wave of vines and then turned and hobbled toward the podium. Before Eli could take more than a few steps toward the podium, one of the vines grabbed his right ankle and leg trying to pull Eli back. Yelling out as the vine's pulling caused the wound in his foot to explode with pain, Eli kept his grip on the rope and trudged toward the podium with the key on it.

The new fear of being eaten quickly helped Eli to push the pain of his body out of his mind and continue his trek to the podium fighting the pulling force of the vines. Eli kept moving forward closer and closer to the stump as other vines wrapped around his other leg and waist. Pol's laughter rang in Eli's ears as the thorns dug into his skin causing involuntary cries of pain.

"Playing hard to get are we?" gurgled Pol. "No matter, I love working up an appetite!"

The strength of the vines increased with every thorny tentacle it was able to wrap around him. Though Eli was fighting with every ounce of strength, his progress toward the podium nearly stalled as Eli could only muster inches forward at a time.

Eli's slowed movement allowed the vine tentacles to start climbing up his body which spurred Pol's gurgling laughter to erupt anew. Soon both of Eli's entire legs were covered by vines as they squeezed and tried to pull Eli back to its mouth. The vine around Eli's waist slowly made its way up Eli's stomach and chest. With only a few feet to go, the vine wrapped itself around Eli's neck and squeezed. Eli could feel his face fill with blood as his windpipes were cut off from their source of life. The thorns in the vine began to cut into his neck and blood poured down his body. Knowing he would not survive to reach the key if he did not do something quick, Eli released his left hand from the rope and tried to pry the vines from around his neck. This tactic worked, and gave him a temporary ability to draw breath, but it also allowed the vine to successfully start to pull him backwards.

I'm losing! thought Eli. *I have to do something quick!*

"Just give in," Eli's flesh's voice spoke into his mind. "No one can overcome his personal desires for joy, pleasure, and riches. The lust of your eyes, lust of your flesh, and the pride of life will conquer you just the way they conquered so many others. Stop fighting! It is easier to just give in. Just let go."

"No!" shouted Eli in a strangled voice.

"No?" asked Pol's gurgling voice. "I think yes!"

Taking a large gasp of what could be his last breath, Eli released the vine, reattached his left hand to the rope and stormed to the podium. Eli stretched his body toward the key. He was mere inches away from the prize, and yet he might as well have been a mile. The vines were draining what little strength he had left and his body was on the verge of shutting down from an overload of pain and a lack of oxygen. Feeling faint with bursts of light popping in his vision, and knowing that his time was down to seconds, Eli poured all of his energy into one last surge. He felt the podium under his hand and then, the key! Eli's fingers found the key and he quickly brushed the key off the podium toward his body. Eli then flung his body on the ground. Now that Eli's feet were off the ground Pol's vines rapidly dragged Eli back. As the vine pulled Eli's body, it pulled his hand right over the key. As his sight began to fade into darkness Eli grabbed the key with his hand as Pol's vines tossed Eli into the air toward his mouth. The last thing Eli heard was Pol's gurgling laughter rejoicing in his victory. Eli blacked out.

When Eli awoke, he found himself lying on a bed that was identical to the four-poster bed he slept on in the castle. The sheets were made of silk and the mattress was so soft Eli thought he was sleeping on a cloud. Eli sat up and was thankful to see his surroundings. The walls and the ceiling of the room looked like a beautiful blue sky and the floor of the room looked like one giant cloud. A refreshing gentle breeze flowed through the room and reminded Eli of the breeze that constantly flowed off of the ocean's waves when he and his family spent a week at the beach. Lining the cloud path from the bed to the door of the room were several beautiful crowns suspended in the air.

Just as it had in the room of fire, defeating the room of thorns had healed all of Eli's wounds acquired from the room. It was as Eli examined his body that the final moments of the challenge became clear to him. As the vine tossed Eli into the air towards its mouth, Eli grabbed the key. Just as in the room of fire, as soon as he grabbed the key, the challenge ended transforming the room and healing Eli's wounds. Even the deep wounds in his foot, thigh, and chest were completely healed. Eli rolled off the bed onto his feet and took several deep breaths of relief.

My flesh was not lying! thought Eli. *This room was intense! I didn't think I was going to make it there for a second.*

A smile etched itself over Eli's face as he thought about his flesh. *I wonder how my flesh is handling the new wounds from this room. I would love to whisper in his head, "just give in."*

Laughing to himself, Eli walked over to the first crown suspended in the air. As he walked on the cloud path, it felt as if he were walking on a giant piece of cotton candy. The first crown was a large golden crown that had a mixture of emeralds, rubies, and sapphires encrusted all around it. In the front of the crown the word "LIFE" was engraved onto the precious metal. Eli reached out his hand to touch it and as soon as his fingers made contact with the crown, Eli's body was instantly filled with power and a verse from the King's Word exploded in his mind.

Blessed is the man

who endures temptation,

for when he is tried,

he shall receive the crown of life,

which the Lord has promised

to them that love him.

James 1:12

Eli fell to his knees as the power that filled his body turned into the most incredible feeling of pure joy. Never had Eli experienced anything like the sensation he felt when he touched the crown of life. After the hurricane of joy subsided inside Eli, he sat on the ground smiling with excited curiosity at the crown and wondering what the other crowns were and how they would make him feel if he were to touch them. Suddenly, the Man's voice from the film sounded in Eli's mind.

"You see, my child, the lust of the eyes, the lust of the flesh, and the pride of life all offer you love, pleasure, happiness, and success. Yet, the one who follows these sinful desires finds only sorrow, shame, and death. I offer you true love, happiness, and success that will last for all eternity, but to attain the great rewards I offer, you must first seek my kingdom with all your being. When you do this, I will add all the love, pleasure, happiness, and success you can imagine in ways that you could never imagine. These crowns you see are just a few of the eternal rewards that I offer to all my children. In order for you to claim these eternal crowns, you must first be willing to set aside the temporary, deceitful desires of this world. It is why I wrote in My Word:

Love not the world,

neither the things that are in the world.

If any man love the world,

the love of the Father is not in him.

For all that is in the world,

the lust of the flesh,

and the lust of the eyes,

and the pride of life,

is not of the Father, but is of the world.

And the world passeth away,

and the lust thereof:

but he that doeth the will of God

abideth for ever.

1 John 2:15-17

"Remember the great contrast between the temporary feelings of joy and pleasure gained from the desires of the world with the eternal feelings of joy and pleasure gained from the mere touch of the rewards I offer for all eternity. When your desires tempt you, think about not only touching these crowns but wearing these crowns for eternity."

The voice ended and the crowns disappeared leaving Eli in the room all alone. Eli knelt quietly for several moments as the rush of joy from the crown and the burning of his heart from the voice of the Man subsided.

"If that feeling is just one of the eternal rewards the King offers to His defenders, I can't imagine the feelings of happiness and love found in the other crowns. I don't know how to earn all of those crowns yet, but I do know that I won't earn any of them sitting in this room."

Eli stood up with the shiny black key in his hand, ran to the door, and exited the room of thorns.

chapter 20
the room of the enemy

Eli walked back into the movie-theatre room and shut the door. Just as the fire door did before, the green wooden door glowed with light that increased with intensity until it disappeared and the door with it. Standing where the door had been was Eli's flesh, now not only covered in burns, cuts, and bruises from the fire room, but also all the wounds Eli suffered from the room of thorns. Eli's flesh did not say anything; he only glared at Eli with an unmistakable hatred before disappearing.

Once again, the glass tiles on the floor lit up a path that led Eli to the black door made out of some sort of skin, with feathers etched into it. Standing in front of the door, Eli realized the skin the door was made out of looked like the skin on the feet of birds. Eli closed his eyes and pictured the scary bird from the film and knew that inside this door, the Enemy awaited him and would likely take the form of the demonic-looking crow.

After facing down the world in the fire room and his desires in the thorn room, Eli was surprised at how terrified he was of what might be waiting for him in this next room. Eli remembered his showdown and conversation with the Enemy back in the cemetery. Eli cringed for a moment at how brash he was toward the Enemy. Eli could be brash and harsh because he was filled with the power of the King's Word and he had the protection of the path. But as his flesh pointed out earlier, the protection of the path did not exist everywhere, and Eli was sure that it did not exist in this next room. If Eli wanted to become a defender and follow in his grandfather's steps, he knew that he was about to face the Enemy, one-on-one, and somehow try to get the key to the final room.

"Do not be afraid, my child." The words of the Man from the film seemed to fill the movie-theatre room. "I have already overcome these enemies, and the Enemy himself. I have given you everything you need to be victorious. You can gain the victory. Do not be afraid of what awaits you. For you to become a defender, you must be able to withstand the Enemy."

As soon as it came, the voice was gone. Its impact, however, remained as Eli's spirit burned with a zealous fire to fulfill his mission for the King. Without hesitating, Eli placed the key in the keyhole and waited for the hologram. As he suspected, the hologram that burst onto the door was the terrifying bird from the film that devoured seeds by the mouthful. The hologram ended, the door cracked open, and Eli marched into the room of the Enemy.

Eli entered the room ready for a fight; his head was up, eyes darting left to right, shoulders tense, and ready to run, fight, jump, and do whatever else survival required of him. The room was not what Eli was expecting. The room was a replica of the field in the film, just giant-sized. The room contained a giant field with the ground plowed into rows separated from the door by a small clearing. On the far side of the plowed rows was a large tree. Hanging from one of the top branches of the tree was a shiny glass key. The only other object in the room was the stone covering over the doorway and two skinny pillars that seemed to spread out where they touched the ground.

No sign of the Enemy, thought Eli as he cautiously peeked out from under the stone cover. "Hello," shouted Eli as he quickly ran to the door waiting for the Enemy to show himself, but nothing happened.

Eli darted out from under the cover and then back under the cover to see if seeing him would draw the Enemy out of hiding, but that did not work either. Finally, Eli yelled out, "No way, I'm leaving," before he opened and slammed the door shut. After a moment of waiting, Eli ran out from the covering, across the clearing, through the plowed field, and took cover at the trunk of the tree.

Again, nothing happened. There were no cries of rage, no movements, and no sign of the Enemy. Confused, but thinking the longer he waited the more opportunity he gave the Enemy to strike, Eli climbed up the tree and out onto a thick branch that could support his weight from which he could reach the key. Eli walked slowly out onto the branch and froze in terror. Standing on the branch, facing the door, Eli got his first actual look at the stone covering with the skinny pillars. What Eli thought was just a covering was actually a stone statue of the giant demonized crow the Enemy appeared as in the film. The pillars that spread out were its legs and talons.

Looking at the key and then back at the statue, Eli wondered if taking the key would make the statue come alive. That thought forced Eli to stop moving and lower his hand from reaching for the key.

"Well now, isn't this awkward!" Eli's flesh's voice laughed in Eli's head. "It looks like the big bad Eli Storm is scared to put his money where his mouth is."

"What are you talking about?" asked Eli even though he knew exactly what his flesh was accusing him of.

"I'm talking about you and your true cowardice. You were all gung-ho to face down the Enemy in the cemetery when you had the protection of the path. But now that your only protection is your own bravery and strength, you are shaking in your boots at the mere sight of my master. Tell me, Eli, where is your faith in the power of the King? Where are those brave words you conjured in the cemetery? Go ahead, Eli, take that key. You know now that taking that key will free my master from his stone prison. Prove to me that I am wrong about you and that you truly are as courageous as you say. If you want to be a defender of the realms, then you are going to have to square off against my master sometime. It is time for you to put your money where your mouth is. Oh man, I am going to enjoy this!"

The voice of Eli's flesh faded away in cruel mocking laughter. Angered not only by what his flesh said but because Eli knew that part of what his flesh said was true, Eli reassessed the situation.

Okay, thought Eli, *I knew the Enemy was in this room and I knew that I would have to face him as the bird. I don't know why I am acting so surprised. By the power of the King I overcame the world and my desires, and by the power of the King I will find a way to overcome the Enemy!*

Taking a deep breath and looking directly at the statue, Eli shouted, "Bring it on!" and grabbed the key.

Immediately a dinner-bell ringing filled the room and a visible sound wave exploded from the base of the tree and spread throughout the room. As the wave passed over the plowed ground giant stone stalks of wheat grew out of the ground. When the sound wave reached the statue of the giant bird, the statue shook and the stone crumbled leaving a giant feather and bone demon-looking crow.

The crow shook itself and spread its wings before looking for and finding Eli in the tree. Eli knew this was the Enemy himself because the eyes of the bird were not bird eyes, but the same eyes of the Enemy he confronted in the cemetery.

"Welcome, Elijah Storm!" called out the Enemy in a shrill cackling voice. "Oh I have been eager for this moment since our little chat in the cemetery. What was it you said, 'It is time for you to run away like the coward you are'? Well, boy, there will be no running away this time. You are here, and you are all alone. Your so-called King has brought you here to be my next meal. Let's see how bold you really are."

The giant bird spread its wings and took flight heading for the tree. Trying not to panic, Eli ran to the trunk of the tree and tried to navigate his path down the tree. Thankfully, the tree had plenty of branches that would slow down if not hinder the Enemy's ability to reach Eli in the tree. Slowly Eli began descending but was nearly thrown down as the Enemy had reached the tree and was shaking the tree with his attempt to get Eli.

Fortunately, the Enemy did not have some supernatural power to hover but still had the limitations of a bird, albeit a giant demon-looking bird. This meant that the Enemy could not stay in one place and attack but had to either fly back into the air or fall to the ground after each strike. The Enemy did not seem too keen on landing and so after every strike, he would ascend back into the sky, circle around and strike again. This allowed Eli some reprieve, and it also gave Eli a plan that would, hopefully, allow Eli to exit the tree without being devoured.

About one-quarter up from the ground, a long skinny branch grew out of the tree. This branch looked skinny enough to bend under Eli's weight but also strong enough to not break. Eli knew it was crazy but he also knew that the Enemy was not going to just let Eli walk out of the room. If Eli was going to survive, then he was going to have to find a way to strike back at the giant bird.

Eli waited until the Enemy struck again and flew back into the air. Sliding down the trunk of the tree Eli landed on the branch and crawled out to the edge of the branch and dangled by his hands. As Eli planned, the branch bent down far enough that Eli could almost put his feet on the ground.

Seeing the situation and thinking that Eli's plan had failed and that he was dangling helplessly off the ground, the Enemy roared in laughter and dove straight for Eli. Waiting for the right time, Eli held on to the branch until the Enemy's beak was within striking distance. Eli released the branch and landed on the ground. The branch sprung back into place and struck the Enemy directly on his beak sending him into a back flip and crashing to the ground.

The Enemy roared in pain and rage. Eli, however, did not stay to gloat, but ran as fast as he could toward the door. Eli made it as far as the plowed field, now full of stone wheat stalks, when a large shadow covered him. Eli looked up to see the Enemy recovered and in a dive with his talons open ready to snatch him. At the last second Eli dove to his right and out of the reach of the Enemy.

Trying to adjust to the limitations of a bird, the Enemy attempted to turn after Eli but wound up crashing into several stone stalks of wheat. The wheat stalks, about five in all, tumbled over into each other and broke into pieces, some of which landed on Eli knocking him to the ground and bruising him.

Again the Enemy roared in pain and rage as he picked himself up off the ground and took flight. Eli's first instinct was to run, but he knew he would not make it. Eli knew that it took him too long to recover and that the Enemy would be able to snatch him up in the clearing between the stone stalks and the door. However, Eli saw a way that he might just be able to buy enough time to survive the room.

In the pile of stone rubble from the stalks, several small caverns were formed in which Eli could fit but not the Enemy. Immediately, Eli ran and climbed under a stalk and into one of the small spaces. Not making a sound, Eli waited to see if his plan had succeeded.

A loud rage-filled scream tipped Eli off to know that his plan had worked. In the time it took the Enemy to regain altitude, the Enemy had lost sight of Eli. Now, hidden under the rubble, the Enemy could not see Eli.

"Do not think you can hide from me, boy!" shouted the Enemy. "I know that you are still in this room. I know that you are somewhere in that rubble and I will find you and feast on your body!"

A ground-shaking thump told Eli that the Enemy had landed close to the rubble pile and loud pecking noises with rubble shifting told Eli that the Enemy was attempting to sift through the rubble to find his prey. Soon the Enemy's beak was reaching under the rubble where Eli crawled and was hammering away trying to enlarge the opening. Eli watched in horror as the beak widened the opening when he saw that by digging under the rubble, the Enemy was actually loosening a large piece of stone stalk that was resting on top of the rubble.

Eli knew what he had to do. Eli knew that he had one more opportunity to strike back at the Enemy and buy enough time to make it to the door, but he did not like what it included. Eli waited for the beak of the Enemy to reach far enough into the cavern that Eli could reach the beak with his legs without being in danger of being eaten.

When that time came Eli kicked the Enemy's beak with all of his strength and began taunting the Enemy.

"Hey little birdie, oh, look at the pretty little bird!" taunted Eli as he repeatedly kicked the Enemy whenever he could.

"You will die the most painful death in all of creation!" shouted the Enemy as he doubled his efforts to break into the cavern.

The renewed vigor of the digging made the stone stalk resting on the bottom rubble even more unstable to the point Eli thought he could push the stalk over. By now, the Enemy almost had his entire head into the cavern. Eli lifted himself up and wedged his back against the rubble and his feet against the stalk that was now visibly unstable. With all of his might, Eli pushed the stone stalk with his legs and it tumbled over the rubble and onto the neck and back of the giant bird pinning him to the ground.

The Enemy hollered in rage as he shook back and forth attempting to free himself. Eli wasted no time; he climbed over the back of the rubble through the opening formed with the stalk gone, and ran full-speed to the door.

Eli knew that if he did not make it to the door, he would not make it out alive. Eli heard the creature free itself from the stock and shake all the debris from its wings, but Eli refused to look behind him. The door was his goal and it was growing closer by the second. Eli reached the clearing between the field and the door when the sound of thunderous wings informed Eli that the Enemy had taken flight.

Twenty yards to go.

"You cannot escape me, Eli! You are mine!"

The sound of the wings stopped which meant the Enemy was in a dive toward Eli.

Ten yards to go.

"Prepare to feel all my wrath and suffer unimaginable pain!"

Five yards to go.

The shadow of the Enemy was directly over Eli.

Reaching the door, Eli swung it open and dove through as the Enemy's talons hit the door, slamming it shut so hard it nearly cut Eli's legs off.

chapter 21
the last room

Eli slid on the glass tiles as the door shook from the impact of the Enemy's talons and what Eli guessed was the Enemy's thrashing against the door to open it. Eli did not know if the door would hold or if the door was soundproof, but Eli scooted back on the ground and was sure he could hear the Enemy's rage-filled screams. Yet, even with the shaking of the door, the same light began to engulf the door and in a short amount of time the door was gone.

Just as it had each time a door disappeared, the room's glass tiles lit a path that led to the next door. This time, however, Eli did not see any sign of his flesh anywhere or in any reflection. Still shaking uncontrollably from how close he came to being eaten by the Enemy, Eli slowly stood and looked at the key in his hand.

"You, sir, nearly got me killed," Eli said to the key. "But I'm sure that you are going to be worth it."

Eli had just defeated every foe he remembered from the parable of the sower and the seed. Further, Eli decided that he must also have defeated his flesh in the process because he did not see his flesh reappear after this last room.

"The Man from the film told me I would have to defeat the world, my desires, the Enemy, and my flesh. I believe I have done all of those so this key must lead me to the way out of this mausoleum and into the ranks of the defenders."

Eli walked with confidence to the door and placed the glass key into the keyhole and turned it. Another hologram burst from the door startling Eli because Eli did not think there would be any more holograms. This hologram was not of some scary test, but was simply a reflection of Eli with a shining helmet floating in the air. The hologram ended and the door cracked open. Not paying any attention to the hologram, Eli walked through the door and into the last room.

The frigid air hit Eli, stinging his face as he stepped into the room and looked around. The room was massive and completely round. The walls of the round room were formed by silently flowing waterfalls descending out of the darkness above and flowing without making a splash into the floor. The floor of the room was covered with a very shallow sheet of cold dark water. The water on the floor and the water lining the walls made the room look like a giant mirror.

The large room was dimly lit with the only source of light coming in the form of a ray from above. The ray of light pointed from out of the darkness above to the top of a large white staircase. At the top of the staircase stood a golden cross with a golden helmet floating above the cross.

"There it is!" exclaimed Eli. "I can't believe it; there it is!"

A rush of adrenalin surged through Eli's body at the sight of the helmet. Finally, the prize Eli had sought for and fought for so diligently was right there in front of him just waiting to be grasped. Eli could not believe it. He had done it; he had followed in his grandfather's steps, and he had heeded the call, overcome the cemetery, and survived all the other rooms. Now, Eli was about to take the helmet of salvation and join the ranks of the defenders.

Just as Eli was about to run toward the staircase, a voice echoed through the room.

"Look what we have here. Elijah Storm walking over to the helmet as if he were actually going to claim it for his own."

Eli froze, instantly horrified by the voice. It was not what the voice said that horrified Eli; it was that the voice was familiar. It was the voice of his flesh.

Turning around frantically looking for where his flesh was, Eli called out, "Where are you? What are you doing here? I thought you were dead."

Laughter echoed off the walls of water and another freezing gush of wind swept through the room, chilling Eli to his bones.

"Dead, you thought I was dead. Oh no, Eli, I do not die that easily. You ask where I am, and what I am doing here. Fool, I am everywhere. What am I doing here? I live here, and so do you. Welcome, Elijah Storm, to your own mind."

Laughter echoed again throughout the massive room as more freezing wind swept through the room stirring the water and splashing Eli with ice-cold droplets. Instead of dissipating, the wind swirled around until it formed a small hurricane in the middle of the room. Water began rising up into the swirling funnel until it looked like a human-size geyser. To Eli's horror, that geyser soon formed into the person of his flesh. This time, however, Eli's flesh showed no signs of the burns, bruises, cuts, or any of the other effects suffered from the previous rooms.

"What happened to all your wounds?" asked Eli, trying to sound defiant.

"Wounds?" asked Eli's flesh in a mocking tone. "I do not have any wounds in here. I do, however, have all the power I need."

Eli's flesh raised both hands into the air and all of the water from the floor exploded up into the air soaking Eli and momentarily blinding him. When the water fell back down, Eli's flesh was gone. Before Eli could find where his flesh went, a painful impact knocked into Eli's back sending him to his knees. Standing behind Eli was his flesh, with an evil grin on his face.

With lightning quickness, or at least he thought it was quick, Eli stood up and sent an upper-cut aimed at his flesh's chin. Eli's punch connected, but harmlessly passed through his flesh's watery face. Eli's flesh smiled and connected another hard punch to Eli's now exposed ribs. Blinding pain shot through Eli's body crumpling him once again to his knees. But his flesh did not stop this time. Feeding on all of his rage Eli's flesh sent punch after punch, and kick after kick, beating nearly every part of Eli's body.

Desperately trying to fight off his attacker, Eli threw everything he had into one punch directed at his flesh's stomach. His fist connected and sank into the body of his flesh. Eli's flesh made a face of agony and then his body of water fell back to the floor.

Thinking he had won, Eli barely had time to smile before his flesh rose up from the watery floor behind him, grabbing his legs and sending Eli face first into the floor of shallow water.

The fall broke Eli's nose causing blood to pour from his nostrils. Thankfully, Eli's flesh relinquished his attack to mock Eli and gloat.

"That was epic!" Eli's flesh mocked. "You should have seen your face. You really thought that you had hurt me. You actually thought that you hitting my stomach was enough to defeat me. Oh man, I can't wait to tell my master how truly weak and powerless you are. I told you, Storm, in here, I have all the power. You cannot defeat me. Heck, you cannot even hurt me."

Wiping the blood from his nose, Eli threw himself up at his flesh. Eli's flesh reached out its hands and he and Eli locked hands in a battle of pushing and pulling. As the two battled, Eli could feel the strength of his flesh.

He is stronger than me, thought Eli. His hands and arms burned with pain as the overpowering strength of his flesh squeezed and pushed.

Eli's flesh pulled Eli's body down and with a quick kick, knocked the wind out of Eli. Gasping for breath, Eli attempted to lunge at his flesh to knock it over. His flesh did not move and once again Eli passed right through his body, falling to the ground. Eli's flesh laughed and landed a painful kick to the side of Eli's leg. Rolling on the ground away from his adversary, Eli had no idea what to do next.

I can't hurt him, but he can hurt me! How am I supposed to win? thought Eli.

Just then a crazy thought popped into Eli's mind and he smiled at his foe.

Eli's flesh looked curious. "Oh really, what are you going to do?"

Eli stood up and ran toward the door and threw his body into the door thinking that the only way to hurt his flesh was to hurt himself. Eli's body crashed against the glass-looking door with a thud. Looking up expecting to see his flesh in agony, Eli was surprised to see his flesh laughing at him.

"You really are pathetic! Did you really think hurting yourself would hurt me? I thought we were smarter than that. I am a little embarrassed in us."

Eli's flesh sank into the water and immediately reformed right in front of Eli. As his flesh rose from the floor, it grabbed Eli by the throat, choking him, and lifted him into the air.

"You are finished, Eli Storm, and you will never get that helmet!"

Eli's flesh threw Eli down and continued his attack. This time the attack came in the form of slow but painful punches and kicks, each one landing where the attacker intended, causing Eli pain. Finally, a powerful punch to the face knocked Eli face down in the water. Eli tried to get up but he was too dazed to do more than pick his upper body up with his arms. Eli heard the footsteps of his oppressor walk up. THUD. Eli's flesh put his foot on Eli's back and pressed him to the ground.

"Do you give up yet?" he mocked. "I told you that I was stronger than you. You cannot defeat me. But don't worry too much. As much as I am enjoying this and as much as I would enjoy prolonging this as long as possible, I have been given direct orders to end you quickly. Apparently, you made my master very angry in the last room and he wants to waste no more time in bringing about your death."

"You and your master are doomed to fail and fall to the King!" cried Eli as he tried to free himself from under the oppressor's foot.

Infuriated, Eli's flesh grabbed Eli's right foot and spun him in the air, laughing insanely.

"How shall I kill you, Eli? Let me count the ways. I could drown you. Yes, that would be fun. I could strangle the life out of your arrogant little mouth. Oh, I would enjoy that. Or, I could simply smash your body to pieces on the staircase. That would be just cruel. Watching you die so close to your goal. Now that I think about it, I think that is exactly what I am going to do."

Faster and faster Eli spun in the air until his flesh released him and sent him flying. After several moments flying through the air, Eli's body crashed into something extremely hard. The impact blurred Eli's vision and caused a surge of excruciating pain to flow through his back. Upon landing, Eli felt his body begin to roll down what felt like stairs. Eli's flesh had thrown Eli into the staircase, just like he said he would. Rolling down the stairs, feeling every shock of pain as the stairs beat upon his body, all Eli could think about was how he had come so close and yet failed. Eli's flesh was right; Eli could not think of any worse torture than to find defeat at the very foot of the stairs of victory.

Eli's body reached the bottom of the stairs and splashed onto the floor. Barely able to move, Eli tried to clear his vision by rapidly blinking as he heard the approaching footsteps of his flesh and the familiar sound of mocking laughter.

Desperate to not give up, Eli rolled over on the stairs to use the stairs to help lift him back up, when he placed his hand on something. Eli looked to see what was underneath him when he saw the familiar shine of silver pages. The sight of his Bible brought back the memory of his grandfather's letter as well as the times in the graveyard when the Scriptures produced the power Eli needed to gain the victory against impossible odds.

"My Bible!" cried Eli. "It must have fallen out when I rolled down the stairs."

Eli saw the pages of his Bible radiating with the familiar light.

Of course! thought Eli. *How could I be so thick? Grandpa told me the King's Word would bring victory when all else fails!*

Eli flashed an intense look at his oncoming foe, who had subsequently stopped laughing at the sight of the Bible. Eli grabbed the Bible and lifted himself to a sitting position on the stairs.

"And just what do you think that harmless book of fables is going to do for you?" growled Eli's flesh. "I told you it takes more than a book with glowing words to defeat me and my master."

"Is that so?" replied Eli. "I think you are wrong. I think that you know that this book has the power of the King. I think you know that it is you and your master who cannot defeat this book. I think that is why you have stopped laughing. Why don't we see just how harmless this 'book of fables' really is?"

"I think not!" yelled Eli's flesh as he extended his arms toward Eli, causing the water on the floor to fly at Eli at incredible speed.

Eli only had time to cover his head and face with his arms to protect them from the wall of water heading his way. But Eli never got wet. Looking up Eli saw that the same glow that illuminated the pages of the Bible had formed a protective bubble around him. The sheets of water were harmlessly bouncing off the bubble.

"What?" cried Eli's flesh in shock. "What is happening? This is impossible!"

"No it's not," replied Eli as he stood up with confidence. "This is the power of the King. Now, STOP!" yelled Eli.

At the sound of Eli's words, the sheets of water fell to the floor. Eli smiled as his flesh, looking utterly terrified, continued to try and control the water to attack Eli.

"Your power is gone," said Eli. "And now it is time for you to die."

"Impossible!" cried Eli's flesh. He turned as if he were going to flee.

"Freeze!" commanded Eli and Eli's flesh's feet and legs turned to ice.

Eli held his Bible in his right hand and concentrated. "How can I defeat my flesh and bury my old man?"

The pages in the Bible exploded with light and turned independently. When the pages stopped, they had opened to Galatians two. As Eli looked at the pages, verse twenty was glowing.

Feeling the power of the King's Word fill him, Eli looked up and spoke with authority, "I have been crucified with Christ; it is no longer I who live, but Christ lives in me. And the life which I now live in the flesh, I live by faith in the Son of God, who loved me, and gave Himself for me."

The King's Word had immediate impact on Eli's flesh. The wounds that Eli's flesh had suffered when Eli defeated the room of fire and the room of thorns were reappearing. Further, Eli's flesh's body was being lifted into the air.

The King's Word turned again to another passage, Galatians five, but Eli did not have to look down to see the verses because verse twenty-four was already filling his mind with power.

"And they," Eli called out loud, "that are Christ's have crucified the flesh with the affections and lusts."

Eli looked up to see his flesh showing all the wounds from the first two rooms. Eli watched as the light from the Bible shot out of the Bible and engulfed his flesh. The light then carried Eli's flesh up the stairs and onto the golden cross, placing him on the cross as if he were being crucified. The same light from the Bible appeared on each hand, on his ankles, on his side, and around Eli's flesh's head.

With Eli's flesh on the cross, another light came from the Bible and lit a path for Eli to walk up the stairs, and then shot into the air and orbited around the golden helmet. Still hurting from the wounds inflicted on him by his flesh, Eli felt rejuvenated as he painfully made his way up the stairs.

As he walked, Eli admired his Bible, the King's Word.

"I can't believe I have had the opportunity to know this book and read this book for so many years and I have simply ignored it."

Needing to hold onto the stair rail to support himself, Eli placed the Bible back into its sheaf and proceeded up the stairs. At the top of the stairs, Eli walked past the cross on which his flesh struggled to be free.

"Wait!" called out Eli's flesh. "You can't just leave me here. I am part of you! You need me. Please, don't do this. You can still go back. We can still have what we once had. Just you and me, please Eli!"

Eli stopped and looked at his flesh. "I don't think so. I remember when we served your master instead of the King and I don't ever want that again! I have been saved! My sins have been forgiven by the sacrifice of the King. I have been given a new life and this life is not mine to live but the life of Jesus Christ who dwells in me. There is no you and me anymore; there is only me and my King.

"You were right though," continued Eli. "I did not survive this mission. The person I was when I entered the cemetery is not the person I am now. I could never have succeeded as I was, but I am not who I was. I am different. My King has defeated you and separated you from me forever. You are defeated and I am new. By the way, if you ever see your master again, let him know that he is next."

Eli's flesh thrashed against his bonds to no avail and opened his mouth to retort, but the light covered his mouth rendering him speechless. Eli smiled, walked past the golden cross and stood in front of the golden helmet.

So this is it? he thought. *This is the helmet that I have come to claim. This is the helmet that will make me a defender of the realms and allow me to serve my King.*

Unable to control himself, Eli laughed out loud. "Let's do this!" he exclaimed and he reached out and took hold of the helmet of salvation.

chapter 22
the throne room

The moment Eli's hand grasped the helmet, the helmet transferred from his hands onto his head. With the helmet on his head, Eli was lifted off the staircase and shot into the air toward the source of the beam of light. It took Eli only a moment to realize that the light that illumined the helmet from above was actually an entrance into a portal.

The portal was just like the portal that took Eli from the atrium to the cemetery; only this time, Eli could relax and enjoy the ride without being nervous of where he might end up. Eli had conquered the cemetery. Eli had gained the helmet of salvation. Eli did not care where he was going or what he would find because he knew with the power of the King's Word, he could face anything.

After a few incredible moments, Eli's feet landed on solid ground and the light that engulfed his body vanished, leaving Eli absolutely in awe. Eli stood in the middle of a room larger than anything Eli ever thought could exist. This room was broken up into three sections by two lines of parallel pillars that ran the length of the room. These pillars were so large, looking up at each pillar reminded Eli of when he visited the Empire State Building and looked up at the building from the sidewalk. The ceiling of this room, if it even had one, was too high for Eli to see. The size of this room captivated Eli but so did the fact that all the materials used in the construction of this room were priceless treasures.

The floors and walls were made out of gold, solid gold! On the gold floors and walls, there were intricate designs carved into the gold, colored using every type of precious stone imaginable. The more Eli looked at the floors, the more he realized the stories of Jesus' birth, life, death, and resurrection were all immortalized on the floor using supernatural skill. The pillars looked like they were all formed from a solid diamond! All of these treasures, and especially the pillars, glowed and sparkled beyond description as the incredible light of the King radiated through the room.

There was also a noise that Eli just started to recognize as he came out of his shock from the portal and from the supernatural magnificence of this room. The noise was the sound of clapping and cheering. Eli looked for the source of the cheering and saw forms of light that reminded him of shadows, only instead of being dark, they were made of light. The forms of light were joined by a host of Angelos and soon Eli saw Michael's massive form walking toward him.

Tears filled Michael's eyes as he approached Eli.

"Well done, Elijah Storm. Well done indeed!" boomed Michael.

With Michael's commendation, the cheering of the light forms and of the Angelos renewed with vigor.

"You have truly honored the King in your victory and have brought glory to His name and excitement to the realm. Your journey to follow in the steps of your grandfather and become a defender of the King is nearly complete. All that is left is for you to be commissioned by the King."

"Wait," said Eli, stunned. "Did you say *The King*, as in the King the King?"

Michael's booming laughter echoed throughout the room and over the cheering that was still going on.

"Yes, Master Storm, I am talking about the King who is blessed forever. He is the One who has called you, forgiven you, empowered you, given you His Word, and He is the One who desires to commission you. Why else would He have brought you to the entrance to His throne room?"

"So that's where we are," said Eli. "It's amazing!"

"Yes it is!" exclaimed Michael. "And you are not even seeing it as it truly is. You see, your vision is still a little limited by your finite mind. However, one day, you will see this room in its true splendor. But enough of that for now. Come, we must not keep the King waiting."

Eli and Michael walked side by side down the middle of the room toward two massive golden doors. As they walked, it was as if Michael could read Eli's mind.

"Do not be anxious, Eli," began Michael. "You have nothing to be afraid of. The King loves you more than you can understand and has not only forgiven your sin but has, as His Word tells us, separated you from your sin as far as the east is from the west. It is He who has called you because it is He who has loved you. There is not a more safe, comforting, or joyful place in all of creation than the presence of the King."

Eli looked up at Michael appreciatively. "Thanks Michael."

Michael smiled back at Eli as the two approached the large doors.

Standing in front of the doors Michael turned toward Eli.

"Elijah Douglas Storm."

"Yes," replied Eli.

"You are about to enter the throne room of the Great King. I will not be going in with you."

"I understand," replied Eli.

"When you enter these doors, you will be met by cherubim and seraphim who will direct you while in the throne room. After you have met with your King, I will meet you here. Now go, and receive your commission from the Thrice-Holy King of all Creation!"

Michael waived his large hands in the direction of the doors and the two large doors silently opened before them revealing a tremendous light. Eli covered his eyes and face and walked into the throne room.

Crossing the threshold, Eli felt a sense of joy and peace greater than he ever thought possible. Warmth of unspeakable proportions filled his heart. Eli had never been more at peace, more joyful, more satisfied than at that moment. The rush of all these feelings combined with the tremendous glory of the light of the room caused Eli to fall flat on the ground. Eli could not get up, but Eli did not want to get up. With everything rushing through his soul, he was most comfortable lying flat on his face in the presence of the King.

After Eli lay there for an unspecified amount of time, he heard loud mighty rumblings followed by the approach of wings. As the wings approached he heard a very calming voice speak.

"Welcome, thou highly favored of the King! Come, for the Great and Thrice-Holy King desires your presence."

Eli wanted to respond but was unable to form any thoughts or words. Eli felt two sets of hands pick him up from under his arms and lift him off the ground. Eli lay limp in their grasp as they flew him further into the room. The joy and peace filling Eli's soul increased more and more as they flew deeper into the room. At last, the creatures lay Eli back on the ground and flew away.

"Elijah Douglas Storm," spoke a great and powerful, yet soothing voice.

The voice was familiar; it was the voice of the Man in the film. Hearing this voice in such personal proximity filled Eli with so much excitement that Eli really thought his being would just explode.

"You have done well, my child. I am so very proud of you!"

Eli's soul nearly shot out of his body as he heard the voice of the King commend him.

"Because of your faith in Me, and your casting off of your old man, you have attained the helmet of salvation. No longer are you responsible for the penalty of your sin. No longer are you a declared enemy of My kingdom. You are now My possession. You are My child, and now I am commissioning you as My defender."

As the King spoke, the helmet of salvation appeared before Eli floating in the air and radiating with a great light. The helmet then flashed and disappeared from the air and reappeared on Eli's head.

"I give you now a mission, My child, to serve your King, your Father, as a defender of the realms against the Enemy. You must continue your training and retrieve the other pieces of spiritual armor from the grasp of the Enemy. As you fulfill your mission, you will bring great glory and honor to My name. To aid you in your quest, I give you a weapon more powerful than the Enemy and any weapon he has: I give you my Word."

Suddenly, the Bible Eli's grandfather left for him appeared in front of Eli, hovering and glowing as the helmet had a few moments ago. The light that had directed Eli's journey through the cemetery and mausoleum and defeated his old man radiated once more. This time, the light engulfed the Bible and in a brilliant flash, turned the Bible into a sword. The sword which now hovered in the place of the Bible, resembled the Bible his grandfather left him in its coloring.

The sword was beautiful. The blade was a double-edged blade made of a brilliant silver material. Wrapped around the blade from the base of the blade to the top of the blade was a thin ribbon of a deep majestic blue. The hilt of the sword was breathtaking. The guard of the sword was a large innately-designed and detailed lion's head. The mouth of the lion was opened with the blade of the sword proceeding out of its mouth. The sword's guard was formed by the top and bottom lion's jaws which extended about four inches out from the blade. On the top and bottom jaws of the lion were four teeth: two on the top and two on the bottom. Each jaw had one tooth on each side of the sword giving it a three dimensional appearance. The teeth of the lion were made of the brilliant silver metal, same as the actual blade. The lion head guard was made of some sort of precious stone with the deep majestic blue coloring with the exception of the lion's eyes which were marked by beautiful sparkling diamonds. The grip of the sword was formed by the lion's mane. The lion's mane flowed down the grip of the sword winding around the grip and connecting to the pommel of the sword. The majestic blue mane wrapped around the shiny silver metal forming a beautiful mix of blue and silver on the grip. The pommel of the sword was a lion's head identical to the guard, only smaller. The mane of the larger lion's head that flowed down the grip connected to the mane of the smaller lion's head which made up the pommel of the sword. The pommel's lion's head was also made of the blue stone with the teeth of the lion made of the silver metal and the eyes of the lion diamonds.

The sword hovered for a moment before landing directly in front of Eli.

"My Word has everything you need to be complete and successful in your endeavors. I personally breathed it into existence and it is profitable for doctrine, for reproof, for instruction in righteousness. If you read my Word, it will guide you. If you trust my Word, it will protect you. If you love my Word, it will bring you great honor.

You have done well already, My child, therefore you have a great reward awaiting your arrival. Go now therefore, and complete your mission. Defeat the strongholds and servants of the Enemy and gain the remaining pieces of armor. Fight the good fight as a defender of the King. Battle the Enemy, free those in his cruel grip. Spread the light of the gospel to those in darkness, teach and disciple those you win, and always remember, I have all power and I will be with you always, even unto the end of the age. I am proud of you, My son, and I love you with an undying love. Go now and bring Me great glory."

Light once again engulfed Eli and he could feel his body being transported out of the throne room. He wanted to cry out and plead to stay in the presence of the King, but he could still not speak. As the light dimmed, Eli was laying on the steps outside the great doors. Eli could see Michael sitting on the stairs next to him, but Eli paused before sitting up. His soul still burned with the joy, peace, and love from and for the King that he had experienced while in the King's presence. Eli wanted to lay motionless for as long as possible and relish in the majestic sensation. As the feeling slowly faded, Eli sat up next to Michael.

"It was incredible!" Eli began.

Michael smiled in such a way that Eli knew Michael understood.

"There is nothing like the presence and majesty of the Great King," spoke Michael. "Come now, there is much work to do. You have a mission to fulfill do you not?"

"I do," replied Eli.

"Then what are you waiting for?" replied Michael as he rose to his feet. "The task awaits us."

Michael extended his large hand toward Eli. Thinking Michael was offering to help him stand up, Eli took Michael's hand. Instantaneously the two were back in the atrium.

Immediately, Eli noticed a change in the room. First, above the gazebo that sent Eli to the cemetery, a large golden helmet hovered. Second, Eli noticed that in the area of the gazebo, the atrium had come to life. No longer was it dark and frozen in time. The atrium area was green, well lit, and had signs of new life and growth. The two streams now flowed through the room and ascended up to the lions' mouths on the other end of the room as Eli suspected.

"You see." Michael laughed. "It is as I said. Your victory in the cemetery brought new life and excitement to the spirit realm. As the atrium attests, life and hope are springing up anew!"

For the first time, Eli realized just how beautiful the atrium could be. Focusing his attention to the other gazebos that stood without a golden piece of armor above them, Eli turned to Michael.

"I bet there are some great adventures waiting through those portals."

"Yes there are, young Master Storm, you can be assured of it," replied a smiling Michael. "The question is, are you willing to pursue those adventures for the King?"

Eli drew his sword from his belt and stared at its majesty. As he looked into the brilliant blade, Eli smiled at his reflection. The person Eli saw in the reflection was not the person Eli was at the funeral. This new Eli was a child and defender of the Great King. This new Eli was a partner with the King's Word, and a co-warrior with the King's servants. This new Eli was not afraid of the world, a slave of his desires, or a prey for the Enemy. This new Eli had fought and defeated his flesh, leaving him in the Cemetery of the Old Man. This new Eli knew that he had a lot of adventures ahead of him and a lot of glory to gain for the King.

Seeing how far the King had brought him in such a short time spurred Eli to respond without having to think too deeply about it.

"That I am, Michael, you can be assured of it."

With sword in hand and Michael at his side, Eli cast a determined look at the remaining gazebos.

"Well, what are we waiting for? I hear there are peoples who need to know there is a new defender in town. I think it is time to share the good news with everyone."

Michael smiled. "Well then, Master Storm, let's begin!"

Also by Nathan D Thomas:

Be Confident in Your Creation

In this book, Nathan shares with you the biblical answer God shared with him concerning God's sovereignty in our lives. Having lost his right eye in a hunting accident when he was a child, Nathan's struggle with his personal creation climaxed when his second child was diagnosed with severe special needs while still in the womb. Broken and seeking comfort, God heard his prayer and opened his eyes to see the truths he shares with you in this book.

Be Confident in Your Calling

A sequel to Be Confident in Your Creation, this book is a study through the book of Hebrews that follows the "let us" calls to action found throughout the inspiring letter. Every believer has a biblical calling from God and this book's goal is to help the believer discover and fulfill that calling.

What's Stopping You?

There are few books in the Bible more applicable to the daily life of modern believers than the book of Proverbs. In this work, originally written to teenagers, Nathan covers seven of the most common pitfalls that keep Christians from living the Christian life they desire to live. It is important to know what is stopping you from living the life you desire because if you know what's stopping you, you can overcome it and move on.

Nathan D Thomas

ABOUT THE AUTHOR

Nathan D. Thomas has a passion for making the Scriptures come alive in a relevant and inspiring way for all ages. Residing in San Antonio, Texas, as a pastor of student ministries, Nathan has dedicated his life to sharing his passion through teaching, preaching, and writing. A multiple published author through Journeyforth publishers in Greenville, SC, Nathan has been burdened by the lack of quality Christian literature for older children and teenagers. Driven by this burden, Nathan has authored the *Defenders of the Realms* series that will engage the imaginations of his readers while sharing powerful biblical doctrine.

Nathan's ministry has taken him all around the world. Nathan has travelled the mountains of Guatemala feeding and ministering in orphanages. He has seen the "impossible" as he led souls to Christ on the streets of a post-Christian London. Nathan has also ministered throughout the islands of the Philippines through teaching, preaching, and performing missionary work. Though his heart is burdened for the peoples of the world, Nathan's passion is to see American children and American teenagers come to Christ and answer the calling to serve the Lord with their lives.

Nathan D Thomas is also a popular event speaker who enjoys speaking at graduations, closing ceremonies, youth rallies, camp settings, and conferences for children, teenagers, and adults. You can follow Nathan's future projects as well as contact him for any future events by following his blog at www.defendersoftherealms.blogspot.com.

Made in the USA
Lexington, KY
28 August 2018